*The Old Man
and the Wolves*

～ *Other works by Julia Kristeva*
published by Columbia University Press

The Old Man
and the Wolves

JULIA KRISTEVA

Translated from the French by Barbara Bray

COLUMBIA UNIVERSITY PRESS
New York

*Columbia University Press wishes to express its appreciation
for assistance given by the government of France through Le
Ministère de la Culture in the preparation of this translation.*

Columbia University Press
New York   Chichester, West Sussex
Copyright © 1994 Columbia University Press
All rights reserved

French edition, Le vieil homme et les loups © Librairie
Arthème Fayard, 1991

Library of Congress Cataloging-in-Publication Data

Kristeva, Julia, 1941–
    [Le vieil homme et les loups. English]
    The old man and the wolves / Julia Kristeva ;
translated from the French by Barbara Bray.
        p.   cm.
    ISBN 0-231-08020-4
    1. Europe, Eastern—Fiction.   I. Bray, Barbara.
II. Title.
PQ2671.R547V5313   1994
843'.914—dc 20   94–11795
                                               CIP

c 10 9 8 7 6 5 4 3 2 1

I resolved to tell of creatures being metamorphosed into new forms.

—*Ovid*

Contents

The Old Man
and the Wolves

Part One

~~~

THE INVASION

1. Whom Is One to Believe? Fear

1

THE WOLVES, driven before the great winds from the north, crossed the frozen river, swept unresisted across the snowy plain, and lurked around the cities for their prey. All through the night the Old Man could hear them howling. He would stand by the window and peer through the mist at their yellow eyes, which shot through with terror the solitude that had built up layer by layer, year by year, in his very skin, his very breath. The panes were covered with the silvery stars, the fretted foliage, the crystalline lace you see decorating store windows at Christmas, made out of tinsel and plastic. But in countries like this one, very hot in summer and very cold in winter, the traceries could be merely frozen vapor. In any event, it was hard for the Old Man, faced with the handiwork of a Santa Claus transformed into a Persian miniaturist, to make out what was going on, and to identify the shapes prowling around the house. But as the ancient green-tiled stove reached its maximum heat, the hoar in the middle of the windowpanes melted, and through the hole the Old Man could descry the drama being enacted outside.

No, he couldn't say he was afraid. Are you afraid when you're merely dreaming, transfixed by something that doesn't exist? Maybe. Yet then your fear is so cold and intangible it seems artificial, a fantasy that's almost entertaining compared with the felt and tragic troubles of mankind. But, dreaming aside, the battle against the wolves was real and permanent: it might be nurtured by night, but it went on all through the day as well. The Old Man was forever coming upon traces left behind by the strange visitors: musky odors mingling with the fug of crowds; claw marks on damp paths in public gardens, and on the throats of animals, birds, and even women. No doubt about it: the savage hordes were here—hidden, but present. They were taking over towns and villages, infiltrating people's very skins. The whole world was becoming more and more canine, ferocious, and barbaric.

"You've been dreaming," Alba Ram would say, smiling.

For sometimes the old man would tell his young friend of his beliefs and his visions. She was the only one in whom he did confide, for although he thought her innocence might doom her to be the wolves' victim, he was sure she would never be their accomplice.

Was it all a dream? Or a nightmare? What was the pain in the pit of his stomach that woke him in the middle of the night, when the howling began again and savage eyes bored through the curtain right into his innards, like red-hot leeches just below his heart? The beasts worried his flesh with their fangs, scoured it with their tongues till the blood was ready to spurt. Waking was no solution now. The wolves had found his weak point and sunk their teeth in. They were tearing him to pieces from within, while outwardly he went on listening to their howls and counting up the tracks they left all over the snow.

2

No one knew his real name. He'd managed things so that his identity card and other papers bore a pseudonym: Septicius Clarus. This sounded rather pretentious, though, if not actually patrician, and as the Old Man hated to embarrass other people he didn't insist on their using it. In private, loyal students of his, like Alba, Chrysippus, and Stephanie, agreed to call him Scholasticus. But he was generally known as the Professor. And Septicius Clarus, aka Scholasticus, aka the Professor, aka the Old Man, used all these aliases to preserve a kind of mystery that became more inscrutable than ever with the advent of the wolves. Unless, that is, their invasion of Santa Varvara unveiled a secret that, though hitherto kept closely guarded, was known to all its inhabitants.

"It must be your ulcer, Professor—your duodenum. Vespasian warned you!" (This from the devoted but skeptical Alba.)

"You may be right, my dear, but it's the wolves that brought it on! As you know, I didn't have it before. So can you tell me why it should start playing up whenever the wolves appear? As for Dr. Vespasian, there's something funny about him. His eyes aren't the same as they used to be. They always were expressionless, but now they're yellow too. Like the eyes of an animal . . . "

"Come on now!"

"Do you remember Chrysippus? I can still see him, always sitting in the front row. And now he's disappeared. Vanished without trace. Who knows, even, if anyone of that name ever existed? Now doesn't that strike you as odd, after we all lived and worked together? You used to spend a lot of time with him, Alba—surely you at least haven't forgotten him? They dragged him away. Devoured him before my very eyes the night they attacked in force . . . "

"Chrysippus was like an alley cat. He'll be back one of these days."

But Alba wasn't as sure as she sounded. That same morning she'd found Epictetus, her angora cat, lying strangled in the garden, with fang marks on his neck and two streaks of dried blood on his fur. She wasn't going to tell the Old Man that, though—it would be more than enough to trigger off his visions again. The neighbors had always been jealous of her beautiful cat, the friend she'd brought with her from her own country—her treasure, her baby. And some people were cruel, that was all. No one liked foreigners, especially female ones, and the natives vented their dislike on whatever the strangers held most dear. No point in going on about it. What was more commonplace than hatred? And they weren't going to upset her, Alba Ram, with their nasty, stupid little murder. No, she wouldn't say anything about it to the Old Man—he had too much imagination. Of course, Chrysippus wasn't a cat. But so what?

"He was my best pupil," the Professor went on. "I tell you—their hatred is different from what it used to be. They're all wolves now! They've been infected. Don't ask me how—my knowledge of science is as old-fashioned as I am, and I can't explain such things. But I can see them clearly enough . . . Still, if even you don't believe me . . . "

She bent over and kissed his wrinkled cheek.

"Good night. Close the shutters, and don't look outside too often. I'll see you tomorrow."

All the same, there was something sinister about the murder of Epictetus. Alba didn't expect charity for a cat that both possessed and deserved other virtues; but that he should actually be killed—that was incomprehensible. As for Chrysippus, better not think about him.

The Old Man was sure what he said was true, and certain that Alba too was aware of what was happening. But experience had taught him that when you tell some people something disagreeable, they think they're doing you a favor if they contradict you. The fact was that when he saw gray-coated, sharp-nosed carnivores slinking singly or in packs through houses and gardens or ferreting in closets, he saw them wearing people's faces and heard them uttering human speech. Some were white and swift and highly bred. Others were more like half-starved curs from the highlands. But they were all from the frozen north and the steppes, and they were all ravenous and without mercy. They would eat carrion if they must, but they preferred a living prey. Farmers had their cattle suddenly snatched away, or found bleeding carcasses and scattered remains. But no one had brought any charges.

"People are frightened, and fear makes them shut their eyes. They prefer to sleep. Otherwise they'd have to gird up their loins and drive the wolves away, wouldn't they?"

The Old Man was telling Alba the usual tale. She was the only one who would stay and listen: others just turned their backs on him with the grim smile habitually bestowed on hopeless cases. But they knew. Everyone knew already. Vespasian had even tried to shoot a white wolf that had settled down in front of his drawing-room fire. For a moment he thought he'd killed it, but it was only wounded, and leaped at his face, tearing away part of his cheek. Then it fled, squealing, and Vespasian was left streaming with blood and petrified with fear.

"There's nothing we can do about them—nothing. We'll simply have to get used to them," he kept saying. He went on like that for several days, as if in a trance. And the Old Man realized the wolf had injected him with its venom.

Yes, people knew, but they said nothing. They just let themselves be poisoned.

3

It was about then that they found the mass grave. Ten thousand officers had mysteriously vanished some time before, leaving no trace.

"The finest flower of the army, of the aristocracy, of the nation!" people whispered. "How could it have happened without our noticing?"

Rational spirits put forward various hypotheses.

"It's the Scythians—only swine like them could commit such a perfect crime! Making men disappear into thin air!"

Skeptics were more cautious.

"But the Scythians were driven out of the country ages ago! Long before this awful thing happened!"

"Who is responsible then? Don't ask me to believe in ghosts!"

"The wolves, I tell you—the wolves! It happened just when they started invading us."

(This was the Old Man, sticking to his guns.)

"There he goes again! Yes, yes, Professor—the wolves, of course! Let's talk about it another time, eh?"

"I can tell you don't believe me. But why not? Just tell me why not! Is there anything improbable in what I say?"

"You really want me to tell you, Septicius Clarus? Well, for a start, nobody's ever seen any wolves in Santa Varvara. Nobody! Just find me one person who's actually seen a single wolf, let alone a pack of them . . . I certainly haven't! And then, even if they really existed, why should the wolves be our enemies? Can you give me a reason? I can't think of one! After all, the wolf is the ancestor of the dog. It can be tamed. Then it will take our side and defend us against its fellow wolves. For there certainly are plenty of other wolves out there in the world! But if we tamed our wolves they'd protect us against the rest—against other people's wolves, if you like. They'd be a kind of defense! . . . No, wolves are perfectly all right if you know how to deal with them—if you're careful not to annoy them, if you give them plenty of room and see that they're happy and comfortable. In a nutshell, if you domesticate them—make them your own!"

Septicius wasn't having this.

"You're the one who's dreaming, not I! Don't you know a wolf never changes its nature? You talk about domesticating them—you must be joking! A few thousand years ago, perhaps. But now? . . . No, you're turning into wolves yourselves—wild beasts fighting against one another. I don't recognize you any more."

"The old boy's obsessed!" (This was Vespasian, showing off in front of Alba and affecting the assurance of the self-proclaimed expert.) "Have you read 'The Wolf Man'? . . . No, but seriously! You can't fool me! I've gone into the subject thoroughly—studied all the books! How many wolves has he seen, that old dodderer of yours? Not five, by any chance? On a tree outside his window? Five—the same number as the fingers on his hand, which he uses for you know what! No, your pal has just been reading too much Freud!"

But Alba loved the old visionary with the trusting and unreflecting love of a little girl, and no one was allowed to make fun of her Professor! Did they have the slightest idea how scrupulous he was?

"You go too far!" she exclaimed. "He never reads anything but Latin! Books in early Latin, late Latin, ecclesiastical Latin—who knows where he's got to by now! People may be starting to be frightened of him, but they still call him the Professor. And as far as I'm concerned, he'll always be my Latin teacher, as you very well know. You say he's been reading 'The Wolf Man'? Why shouldn't he? But I'd be surprised, myself. I'm sure he considers Freud too seductive, too frivolous."

"Freud—frivolous!" Vespasian sounded meaner and more pompous than ever. "But say what you like, that's the explanation!"

4

So the mass grave was found in the mountains, at the bottom of an old, disused quarry. On the sullied limestone five thousand bodies lay heaped together —bitten into, gnawed, mutilated. There were bullet marks on the walls of the grave, and, beside it, rifle butts covered with scratches; teeth; blood.

"The Guards were the only ones who could face up to the wolves. They must have realized the danger before the Old Man did, and organized a great drive, in secret, to expel the invader."

"And the wolves lured them into a trap and blocked the

exits. You couldn't aim at anyone in particular in the dark, so they just slaughtered them like chickens!"

"But they didn't go without a fight. Look—there are wolves' bodies mingled with the those of the soldiers."

"Five thousand men! How horrible! . . . But where are the others? There were ten thousand men in the Guards, weren't there?"

"Perhaps the rest escaped and are organizing resistance abroad."

"Do you think so? I've never heard of anyone opposing the wolves. Except, of course, the Old Man—but is he really a member of any resistance? I'd say he was more a prophet, a sensitive plant, a visionary."

"So?"

"So the wolves killed the rest as well! Every wolf dragged one or two corpses away to its stinking lair. To stock up for the winter. The Frozen North is a very harsh place, you see— there's nothing to eat there—so they come here and strip us of our best possessions: our food reserves and our men. And now, it seems, they actually come and live in our houses."

"Perhaps we'll find another mass grave later on, somewhere else."

"Who can say? And what good would it do you to know too much about it? Come on, let's go back."

Then came disaster: out-and-out invasion. The Old Man, overcome with horror, withdrew into his own aura of wisdom and honor, which no one was intelligent enough to name—or brave enough, which amounts to the same thing. But they all intensified his isolation with their hints, their furtive looks, and their servile gestures. The whole country, frozen with fear and compromise, was shrouded in the kind of silence where the just are lonely and the rest reek of hypocrisy. The Old Man went on keeping watch from the window, his stomach racked with pain. But strangely enough it was his suffering—a wolf's den within his own flesh—that saved him, for his unwavering vigilance seemed to prevent the barbarians from approaching his house. Suffering is the banner of the weak, a radiance that wards off degradation.

2. Nothing—That's What He Thinks

1

OAKS, MAPLES, and beeches—scarlet, vermilion, and ocher—surged up the mountainside like fire. Septicius Clarus was savoring his seventieth autumn through greedy, melancholy eyes. The pleasure he got from the bright-hued season was that of taste and touch. All the shades of brown and yellow and red entered into his skin, warmed his throat, filled his eyes, inducing the overwhelming sense of fulfillment that cannot be adequately expressed except in song. But he wasn't going to sing now: pleasure was looked down on in this country as if it were a kind of madness. Instead he went over to a frail tree with cherry-colored leaves and shook it gently, bringing down a shower of sweet-smelling tongues of flame. This was a habit of his, which used to amuse his daughters greatly, long ago, before they left the land of the wolves: "Papa, do the fall! Papa can do the fall!" Amid this cool arboreal conflagration, they would laugh, and he would be warmed by their laughter. But that was a long time ago.

Where are we, then? In a forest in the state of New York, near the Canadian frontier? In some wild spot in the Carpathians? In the mountains of northern Greece, where Orpheus pursued his Eurydice? The Old Man hadn't forgotten that he was in Santa Varvara; at home. He also knew that reason had the mysterious power of letting anyone be anywhere. Yet he was well aware that despite the riot of sylvan color transporting him into another world, events very much of this one were taking place around him, imposing a burden on remote Carpathians, mythical Greece, and North American forests alike. A burden of murder. The ferocity of the wolves.

At mihi parce, Venus: semper tibi dedita servit/ Mens mea; quid messes uris acerba tuas?—"But to me, Venus, be merciful: I am your ever-faithful servant; why should you cruelly destroy your own harvest?

"Neither forget the feasts of Adonis, mourned by Venus, nor the religious ceremonies performed on the seventh day of the week by the Jews of Syria . . . "

Some lines of Latin poetry slipped in amongst the leaves. Their resonance reconciled Septicius with lost time. The sensual, almost degenerate self-assurance that he'd loved so much and recited and taught so often! These verses belonged to the end of a world, the end of the Roman world, which existed before us just as we exist now before some new barbarism or some mere metamorphosis: whatever it was, the Professor was trying to face up to it. But here and now, beneath the flames of fall, he found himself overwhelmed yet again by the lost magnificence. No doubt about it, he would always belong to that world of long ago that he called civilization.

"Just keep away, dark Death, your eager hands—keep them away, grim Death, I beg: I have no mother here to gather up my incinerated bones in the folds of her mourning veil; I have no sister to bestow on my ashes the perfumes of Assyria and weep with unbound hair beside my grave."

Young Tibullus again, making one's eyes brim over with his elegies! Sad, many-faceted Tibullus; anticipating Christ? But Tibullus's Christ, if he'd ever lived, would have died without the illumination of grace. How many years before the coming of the Resurrected One did he live—twenty or so? Everyone has forgotten him now. The pupils in the Professor's Latin class, who quite enjoyed their elderly teacher's fads, used nonetheless to laugh up their sleeves when he assumed the voice of the amorous poet, that ancient Romeo, first smitten with the lovely Delia, but then transferring his oratorical ardors, and no doubt his physical ones as well, to a fetching youth called Marathus. Honestly! . . . Those young footballers and water-polo players couldn't have cared less about the emotions, or the rugged verses, of Tibullus, Ovid, or Prudentius: a lot of boring old egg-heads! Old Septicius didn't seem to realize how much what he called "civilization" had changed. Oh well. Let him amuse himself in his museum. He wasn't a bad old stick. But why was he there? What on earth was the point of keeping Latin on the syllabus in the age of computers, compact discs, space probes, and word processors?

But he understood them well enough, the old eccentric. He noticed their pitying laughter. But he pretended not to. Because if people perceive that civilization is over and done with, then it really *is* over and done with. At least, that's what he thought at the time. And he went on reading them Tibullus.

"As for me, may my poverty allow me to pursue my leisurely life, as long as the fire glows constantly on my hearth . . . And may I myself, like a real farmer, plant with skillful hand and in proper season the tender vine stock and the young fruit tree . . . For I honor deeply both the old tree stumps that lie buried in the fields and the ancient stones still standing at the crossroads, garlanded with flowers. And the first of all the fruits that spring bestows I lay at the feet of the country god . . ."

2

Whereas what his contemporaries liked about Rome moving toward decline was its rank atmosphere of unconscious decay, its languid indulgence in squalid display, insipid debauch, and unsated lust for pleasure, Septicius Clarus was interested in any pointers the period might contain to its problematical future. Not that his Ovid and his Tibullus had anything in common with the anxious slaves who dreamed of a Savior—those modest but sublime imitators of the orgies of Pompeii who offered up their bodies for a martyrdom invented earlier by pagan gods but now dispensed by priests infuriated by the advent of a spirit from Judea. A ghost who proclaimed himself the One True God. No, all Septicius sought to do, via metamorphoses and elegies set down in a dead language that he rehabilitated, was to create a kind of music. One that, like all the most marvelous sounds, emerges from a brutish cacophony, refining it into duration, expectation, and promise. The promise of harmony, perfection. Epiphany.

He saw this transition in the changing shapes that filled the pages of Ovid, transforming an incestuous girl into a sweet-smelling shrub, a murderess into a bitch, an egoist into a flower, an amorous sister into a river, a group of randy ladies into trees, a king into a woodpecker, a town into a heron, Caesar into a star—but not yet a man into God. For while the changes that took place in Ovid were punishments—or, at the very least, tokens of disapproval—the being who imposed them seemed to take as much pleasure in the obloquy of the offense as in its chastisement. Was his intention to wipe out the sin, or to immortalize it?

Ovid and Septicius hovered somewhere between the two, on the edge of indecision, of the baleful human condition that hadn't yet chosen its cross but already overflowed with passion. As for Tibullus, steeped in love, he fed Septicius sweetness like a ripe fruit that knows it must rot but still gorges itself to bursting on the sunshine. The elegies sing of infinite death. They drink deep of death, they grow drunk on it, but they don't believe in it; for them there is no quietus. Does Tibullus know he's waiting for a Christ to open up eternity?

Septicius, a parent himself and an orphan, didn't really set much store by an eternity provided by a Father: to both the implacable grave and the resurrection of the Gentiles, he preferred the inconsolable Tibullus. Neither decadent nor optimist, the Professor saw himself as standing on a dividing line: as a bone between two cavities, a boat between two waves, always eager for the turmoil that affords a glimpse of the worst, the vortex that throws up the strange images in which philosophers may later read truths. Nevertheless, bone or boat, Septicius knew the present was a period of transition. So he looked at Santa Varvara through the eyes of Ovid and Tibullus.

3

Some of his pupils yielded to the charm of the period, a time of maturity, mingling fulfillment and intimations of death. They repeated those dreamy, inspired verses as if the language of Rome had never been forgotten; as if by some mystical metamorphosis the elegiac melodies of Latin youth had entered into their tee-shirted bodies.

"And the first of all the fruits that spring bestows I lay at the feet of the country god . . . "

That was Alba, of course: the most gifted, the most severe, yet the most luxurious embodiment of a general enthusiasm that, though nostalgic, was also alive and invincible. No, Rome was not dead—it had undergone a metamorphosis and taken on new forms. Barbaric ones, you say? Perhaps. New, at all events. Unadorned clay pots. But weren't the first goblets, too, made of malleable earth?

Alba, living like Septicius in a country invaded by wolves, shared his passion for Rome, but without going to extremes. She shared it almost out of shyness; certainly out of politeness. But hers was a thoughtful courtesy, the keen curiosity of the disappointed.

She was obstinate and ambitious, however, and said she preferred Suetonius. The *Lives of the Twelve Caesars*, written in the reign of Hadrian, was the work of a sort of gossip columnist who cast on the greatest men in Roman history an eye sometimes caustic and sometimes impassive, but always completely immoral. As in Santa Varvara now, so then in Rome, an age was drawing to a close without anyone noticing—not even Suetonius himself, typical though his relativist attitude was of the end of an era. His work was devoid of irony or reproach, sentiment or hope. Seen from within, corruption and "business," vice and virtue, all balanced one another out; probabilism—a kind of pragmatism based on the theory that there is no certain knowledge—became the religion of the superstitious sages. If there'd been any people living then who had an inkling of coming invasion, thought Alba, they must have been like Suetonius. Plutarch's hero worship struck her as anachronistic; Tacitus still believed history had a meaning; but Suetonius merely related physical weakness elevated, for better or worse, to positions of greatest political power. Minimalism, usually so abhorred, is the amoralist's morality. If Alba had followed the Professor's predilections, she would have embarked on the umpteenth thesis on Suetonius. And who knows, she might have struck some original sparks out of the subject, found some aspect in it that was relevant to the present. But Alba wasn't enough of a student for that. Moreover, she believed that modern Santa Varvara might shed light on Roman history, but not vice versa. The present, however, was both crushing and elusive, and Alba preferred to concentrate on its cookery: so she would sandwich a few pages of Suetonius between an hour in the kitchen, preparing a shoulder of pork cooked with fifty cloves or a dish of salmon trout flavored with ginger. The Suetonius was due partly to gratitude to Septicius, partly to compulsion—but compulsion grows out of gratitude.

"There then prevailed in the East an old and persistent belief that, in accordance with certain predictions, some people would at this time come forth out of Judea to take possession of the whole world and rule over it."

These words were written in the first century A.D. Did any of those "old and persistent beliefs" still survive? Perhaps some people were even now in the process of rising up, getting ready to take possession of the whole world and rule over it. Would that be a good thing, or not? Did anyone know who they were? Was there a modern Suetonius? No, history didn't repeat itself, and predictions were all worn out. Silence was the only valid art. The only art of living. And Alba would return to her shoulder of pork cooked with fifty cloves—or her trout flavored with ginger—and prepare to face Vespasian's bad temper, which was merely a mask for his mental confusion.

What was she looking for? That mixture of grandeur and perversity, depravity and integrity quite absent from Santa Varvara, which had nothing to show but apathy and self-abasement? A Julius Caesar who was "lover of all wives and mistress of all husbands," and who boasted that "his soldiers could fight even while wearing perfume," was Julius Caesar still, perhaps even more so. Then there was the strange case of Augustus, stripping a Roman knight of his possessions and ready to sell him into slavery because he'd had his two sons' thumbs cut off to save them from military service. And what intransigence!—boldly proclaiming that "what is done well is done fast enough," and offering his own daughter to serve as a Vestal Virgin when he was really about to exile her for debauchery. "His body was said to be covered with sores and callouses from his scratching himself with a scraper, and there were birthmarks like the constellation of Ursa Major strewn all over his chest and stomach." So the divine Augustus was in fact quite an abject figure. He forced one of his favorite emancipated slaves to kill himself because he'd been discovered in flagrante delicto with various Roman matrons, and ordered Thallus, his secretary, to have his legs broken for selling the contents of one of his master's letters for fifty deniers. But delight in duplicity and crime reached its apogee in the reign of his successors, Caligula and Nero. Now Alba could relish vice on the grand scale: "Gaius could no longer restrain his penchant for cruelty and evil, watching with eager curiosity the torture and execution of prisoners, and going out at night to brothels and other places of ill repute, disguised in a long robe and wig."

For it wasn't the absence of morals that shocked our perfidious young historian, but triviality. And while the Caesars were excessive and immoderate, Santa Varvara's way of going on, though brutish enough, was merely mean and small-minded. As for the auguries and other omens that Suetonius relied on, Alba, as superstitious as she was perverse, couldn't help being fond of them. The Professor didn't care to think that his best pupil was secretly attracted to a Roman historian who dealt in poisoning and lust, treachery and repression. The suspicion did occur to him, but he wouldn't dwell on it; for when everything appears to be corrupt you can't help valuing whatever at least takes the trouble to seem respectable. As did Alba, unwittingly in the grip of a guilty passion doomed to emerge some day into the open. But we mustn't anticipate.

4

The thing was to remain lucid beneath those crimson leaves, while wolves scoured the plain and no one remembered Tibullus, Ovid, or Prudentius any more. Except perhaps Alba, when she'd had her fill of Suetonius's porno thriller. And of course Septicius himself, separated by his books from a world without light.

But there was still Nature, its sap full of vigor even at autumn's end. "But soon death will come, its head shrouded in shadow, and soon will come numbing age."

Rhythmic prose, poetry turned into narrative, the ordinary expressed with simplicity—that was enough for the Old Man. Even when he closed his eyes the mirth remained: the universe was so rich in the fall that a mere story, a tale told in two lines, could transform perceptible time into fantasy, but a fantasy that always had a human face. The Old Man's mind, whether working fast or drowsily, juggled with confessions, images, and destinies. The bustling crowd of metamorphoses divested itself of matter: "*sine materia, exercitium arithmeticae occultum nescientis se numerare animi.*" It was a kind of airy music, which carried him away.

Indian summer had come, and the Professor didn't go up to drown in the riot of color until the first snaps of cold tweaked off the leaves and dropped them gently into his hands or before his feet. Nothing would have induced him to pick them himself: to tear off those sublimely dying branches would have struck him as uncouth. So, leaving children and lovers to hack off the scarlet swathes, he went down the coast.

5

Now the Old Man and his eternal shantung suit were to be seen in a seaside resort given over at this time of year to senior citizens and a few wealthy foreign couples. In the hotel lobbies all the sofas and armchairs were swathed in dust-sheets. In every bar a solitary barman played his favorite tango over and over again to relieve his boredom and make up for the lack of customers. The Old Man had learned not to hear most of the local noises, but even he stirred to the vibrato of Billie Holiday singing "Some men love me 'cause I'm happy." Caught out in such modernity, he would smile awkwardly. Fancy an old stick-in-the-mud like him enjoying that inspired, suggestive, flesh-and-blood, milk-chocolate voice. Some odd fish of a former guest, a jazz lover, had—in return for some courtesy or other, unusual in this uptight country—bequeathed the barman, together with a pair of jeans and some trainers, a couple of scratchy old records.

In the darkness the empty dance floor seemed insubstantial, like the almost insensible white film covering an unhealed wound. Foreign voices rustled under the lime trees; the rich couples must be speaking German or Russian—it didn't matter which, the two went well together. But the Old Man enjoyed trying to identify the wordless laughter punctuating the broken phrases: the plump laughter of ponderous Slav ladies, which gathered and gurgled for a long time in their mouths before dying out at last in their stomachs; the solemn and distinguished whipcrack of Germanic male gullets.

He recognized his compatriots, the pensioners of his own country, by the threadbare jackets of the men and the dark-ringed eyes of the women: they were all prematurely worn and damaged. *They* didn't speak. They hunched over their plates without even looking at one another, for a glance might suddenly extract a few words from you, even against your will. Sometimes a blue-veined old hand would rise from the tablecloth to stroke a wrinkled arm. Were they afraid? Those colorless, shapeless bodies with minds that knew nothing and now didn't want to know . . . They were not so much stupefied or bemused as seized by a kind of numbness, by the guilty pleasure of someone taking a warm bath after the water has been cut off. "What are we doing here amongst these strangers? Are we in some sort of limbo?"

The Old Man bothered them even more than he did the heedless tourists. Admittedly he'd given up talking to them about the wolves: he'd soon been given to understand that what he had to say on this subject was if not actually untrue then at least uncalled-for. Septicius had got the message: he wouldn't say anything. But wasn't he exasperating enough in himself, with his reproachful looks? And they didn't even carry conviction! For as soon as he forgot or thought himself unobserved, he would slip back into his usual blissful expression, like the look worn by saints in the now disused churches. That was it—he must take himself for a saint, with his half-mournful, half-ecstatic silence, his shantung suit, and the old-world elegance he flaunted on the empty dance floor, going so far as to kiss the hands of elderly lady pensioners who didn't know whether to be flattered or furious. Fancy kissing hands wrinkled with age and detergents while the wolves were everywhere—at least according to him, and everyone knew he was right, even if they didn't want to get drawn in!

"If you want to know what I think, my dear," an old guy would whisper to his wife, in bed and far from the prying eyes of the barman or the foreigners, "I think talking about this sort of thing—the wolves, I mean—only makes them more real: you have to believe in them, and so you have to do something about them. Or else do nothing. But that's the whole problem. It's much better not to talk about it. What is there to say, anyhow? It's just life, isn't it? Do you see what I'm driving at?"

"He's just trying to provoke the wolves, that's all. Our hero must be starting to get bored with his books!"

"Obviously! Good night!"

The Old Man himself didn't go to bed till dawn, after the Germans and the Russians, who waited till midnight before making the occasional sally on to the scarlike dance floor. Not until they'd gone upstairs would he start badgering the barman again with his idée fixe about the invaders. Eventually the barman entered into the spirit of the thing, and there they would remain until the still invisible sun turned the east indigo, the pair of them singing along hoarsely and gleefully with Billie: "Maybe I'm a fool but it's fun," "I'm happy to do what I'm doing for you," "My mother, she give me something," "I have a long long way to go," "Nights full of passion, jealousy, and hate."

"You're lucky, being able to understand what she says." (The barman.)

"I only understand a few words here and there." (The Old Man.)

"But I've heard you say, 'Baby won't you please come home?' and 'I'll never smile again.' I can say the words too, you see—but what do they mean, exactly?"

"They mean that other people bore me, I don't want to listen to them, and that your girl, on her record, is a whole different world. The future of the past. There is such a thing as light seriousness, don't you agree?"

"I don't know about that . . . But I agree that she's a different world all right!"

And then, in the now pink-tinged rays of dawn, they'd both start singing "On the sunny side of the street" again, while the wolves assembled behind the neighboring dunes. That shrill, voluptuous voice, invigorating as the ocean, innocent as the coquetry of a little girl, rasping with pleasure and pain, languorous, demanding, bitter . . .

"Yes, monsieur, you're right—there *is* another world. There are other things beside wolves, don't you agree?" (The barman, insistent.)

Nothing—the Old Man didn't think anything. His body, in its shantung suit, was already heading for the sweet-smelling oleanders on the other side of the garden, then for the darkened lobbies and their shrouded furniture.

6

Suddenly he saw a thin but well-shaped arm, the nimble arm of a young woman, tucking a stray lock of fair hair into her chignon. Was it Alba? He was having another hallucination. Was it the arm of his daughter, his youngest daughter, whose fingers were hardened from stopping the strings of a violin, who often tucked back her hair too, but hers was black, and she sometimes wore it in a braid around her head? That slim arm lifting the tresses to reveal a nape covered with corn-colored down—he'd dreamed about it ever since his daughter went abroad to be a celebrity. Ever since his wife died. Ever since he'd been left alone with his books—long before the wolves came. He'd described it, preserved it in the novel he was forever tirelessly unfolding in his head; a novel that would never become a book, but that he was forever reshaping in accordance with his dreams, his sleepless nights, his worries.

It was one of those nights when the stars disappear behind the clouds or evaporate into the iodine-steeped air breathed out by the wrack of stormy tides. A warm night, perfumed by natural smells at once intoxicating and sickly, on the boundary between germination and death. The senior citizens had been asleep for a long time; the foreigners had followed. Only a few of the most mellow Russian and most energetic German couples still jostled one another on the dance floor, either under the sway of sentiment or from a sense of duty.

In his slacker periods, which tended to be more and more frequent since his retirement and became especially oppressive under a sultry sky, the Professor wrote *Prata*—his "Meadows," as he called them to a few chosen initiates among his students, including Alba and Stephanie. These learned but apparently disorganized outpourings brought together a number of epiphanies gleaned in the light of leaves and waves, but especially during daydreams of the young violinist who was giving the benefit of her name and grace to some far-off world in which she had forgotten him.

A half-formed image of life. A fleeting snatch of the ephemeral. The awkwardness of the sketch foretold the death of an apparition no sooner glimpsed than lost. These incomplete tales were really elegies.

For instance:

"The fingers, their violinist's nails cut square with the fingertips, lift the hair off the nape of the neck; the black coronet is wound around the head; and the arm, tense in its unconscious, automatic effort, bends in a fragile arc; a tamed serpent; a music of many fibers."

No, that's not it. Let's try again.

"Her thick hair hangs down her back, her hands rise up like gulls' wings. They divide the mass into three parts, weave them into a braid, revealing little pink ears like a baby's. The moonlight quivers on the amber skin of arms unconscious of what they are doing."

No, still not right. The *Prata* aren't any good tonight. What's more, his daughters were dark: their jet-black hair could never have belonged to that fair arm patting its head, the arm of a girl in a mauve blouse and a tight tobacco-colored skirt, over there under the lime tree.

No doubt about it. It really was Alba Ram. But at this hour?

"Vespasian will soon be here. He wants to marry me." (Alba.)

Septicius Clarus didn't bother to show surprise. Nothing. That's what he thought. Nothing.

"My parents have disappeared." (Alba.)

Nothing. The barman was beginning to be curious.

"Father was a member of parliament, as you know. For the South."

"The wolves have already reached the South." (The Old Man.)

"Is it enough just to be a member of parliament—for that to happen?" (The barman was sticking his oar in.)

"There's always a struggle between the Old and the New Régime." (Alba.)

"When people panic beyond a certain point they don't have a nationality any more. They even forget to be racists." (The Old Man.)

"The wolves never panic. They cause panic in others, and wreak havoc in their souls. Souls are more vulnerable than nationality or race." (Alba.)

"Yours is an acquired simplicity. It's not natural." (The Old Man.)

"Tears bring me back to daylight." (Alba.)

"It won't be daylight for a long while. Don't you see how dark it is?" (The barman.)

"You've become quite indifferent. But that makes people curious. And they get annoyed if they can't make you out." (Alba to the Old Man.)

"One can't go on indefinitely living off the sight of a forest blazing with color in the fall." (The Old Man.)

"My parents have disappeared . . . Did I tell you? I watched a woman changing into a muzzle, a pair of jaws, an animal. I still had a look, an expression left that might have saved her. But by then she wasn't capable of sparing anyone else a glance." (Alba.)

"Yet one can still have a feeling of happiness, as if your heart were being kissed by a woman you love." (The Old Man.)

"What are you talking about?" (The barman.)

"Everyone is running away." (The Old Man.)

"Vespasian wants to marry me. What do you think?" (Alba.)

At that point Vespasian joined them, leaving the porter to take his baggage upstairs.

"What a surprise!" (He was obviously put out to find the Professor here.)

"What do women want, Scholasticus?—You're having a good holiday, I hope?—Marriage, of course! It was Alba's idea ... I couldn't care less! ... Just the sort of idea a woman would have." (Vespasian.)

7

The Old Man didn't bother to comment. Nothing. He wasn't thinking anything.

"Well ... It's an idea ... whoever thought of it ... It's not done to ask an idea where it came from. The thing is that it exists." (The Old Man is acting like a professor again, but he can't bring himself to say "Congratulations!") "It's a good thing, a very good thing, that an idea *should* exist. It happens so rarely. But it changes other ideas, changes *things* retrospectively. And in the present circumstances ... "

"You're not going to start on those wolves of yours again? You admit there *aren't* any wolves here, don't you?" (Vespasian.)

"You can't see anything on a night like this ... You can't see them." (The Old Man.)

"I was sure of it! ... Are there many people here?" (Vespasian.)

"Tourists and old folk." (The Old Man.)

"No one to speak of, in short. Just what we need." (Vespasian.)

"We've fled from the city too." (Alba.)

Nothing. The Old Man wasn't thinking anything.

"Let's not exaggerate. We needed a rest. Just an ordinary trip to celebrate an engagement." (Vespasian.)

"There's no such thing as an ordinary trip to celebrate an engagement . . . Honeymoons, yes . . . " (Alba.)

"All right—I've invented it! I have a perfect right to do so, haven't I, my friend?" (Vespasian to the Old Man.)

Nothing. He doesn't think anything.

"The people in town are turning nasty—insulting and denouncing one another. Just like wolves." (Alba.)

"Still at it? My dear, you're imagining things. They've found a mass grave? Right! Mutilated corpses? Just so! But why should the wolves be held responsible? It might have been . . . I don't know . . . pigs, wild boar, bats, rats . . . " (Vespasian.)

"I'm talking about the people in the street, on the street-cars, in the shops, in the hospital. Their faces have changed." (Alba.)

"It all depends how you look at it." (Vespasian.)

"My parents have disappeared." (Alba.)

Nothing. The Old Man didn't think anything.

He looked again at the fair arm as it moved beside the mauve blouse and reached for the glass of ice water that the barman had just set down on the table, together with two glasses of beer. She took a sip and lifted her arm again, this time to undo the fair braid wound around her head. Her hair then fell down about her shoulders in the dry water of the neon. In such a light, his own violinist's hair looked green, and her muscular arm was coffee-colored. "The best thing I ever did was to get my daughters out of hell," he thought. But he didn't say it, because of Alba, and even more because of Vespasian.

"It's hell," said Alba.

"My dear, if you take that attitude even before I've married you, the future looks decidedly bleak." (Vespasian.)

"I'm talking about something else." (Alba.)

"You sound as if you're all running away." (The barman was

definitely taking liberties now—because of Billie Holliday he saw himself as the Old Man's buddy.)

"What an idea!" (Vespasian.)

"Yes, in a way." (Alba.)

"We're here for a breath of sea air." (Vespasian.)

"But it's very close here, too." (Alba.)

"It comes and goes."(The barman.)

"Not too many guests?" (Vespasian.)

"Some Germans and Russians." (The barman.)

"Some senior citizens too." (The Old Man.)

"I'll say!" (Vespasian, crossly.) "Can we dance?"

"No law against it . . . It does happen." (The barman.)

"I love tourists, really. They take things easy, they want to enjoy life. The people at home are all defeatists now. The place is like a morgue!" (Vespasian.)

"Are you a doctor?" (The barman.)

"Yes. Why?" (Vespasian.)

"Your way of looking at things. Detached. Like an X ray. Ruthless. I mean, you know it all." (The barman.)

"I should hope so. It prevents me from taking a man for a wolf. Ha ha! Isn't that so, Scholasticus?" (Vespasian.)

"Some men turn into wolves." (Alba.)

"My wife—my future wife, that is—is very sensitive, as you'll have noticed. And the charm of the melancholy type is well-known. All too well-known. Limited, though . . . Oh, but I do love women, old boy—there's no getting away from it. Can you imagine a finer sight than a beach full of women?" (Vespasian.)

"They're a bit strange now, though." (The barman.)

"What do you mean?" (Vespasian.)

"They're rather abrupt and rough, to my way of thinking. Like everyone else, in fact!" (The barman.)

"That's what gives life its savor, my friend! But we'll talk about it later. Come along, Snow White—beddy-byes. Tomorrow is another day." (Vespasian.)

She kept on raising and lowering her arm, braiding and loosening her hair. Nothing. The Old Man didn't think anything. The engaged couple disappeared into the clammy, seaweed-smelling darkness.

"She looks as if she's running away, but not with him. How far will she get, though, if he keeps trailing after her?" (The barman.)

It was so dark the illuminated scar of the dance floor was no longer visible.

"She's looking for her parents—they've disappeared. She doesn't know where she's going. Do you?" (The Old Man.)

Nothing. The barman didn't think anything any more.

Then suddenly the shadows under the arbors and amidst the clumps of acacia bordering the terrace seemed to take on animal shapes. There were swarms of lurid heads: gaunt skulls with gaping mouths, fierce eyes peering from bushy manes, flying bodies, glimpses of bone. And the whole purgatorial vision was lit by flashes of lightning.

"Here come the bats again. On stormy nights the seaweed upsets them." (The barman, unperturbed.)

8

The Old Man was at his usual post by the window. A shattering peal of thunder was followed by a flash of lightning that revealed some terrified peasants hiding behind a sand dune, watching in terror as a wolf, pen in hand, wrote out their death sentence. A short distance away a chestnut horse was being attacked by a famished pack. The horse whinnied, struggled with all its might, but the beasts from the steppes swarmed all over it, tearing at its neck and hindquarters, devouring its legs and belly. The sheep dogs just looked on in amazement. Soon there was nothing left of the horse. But what a fight it had put up! No man could have withstood such an attack.

The storm passed over, again the hotel was shrouded in darkness, once more all was invisible. The Old Man folded his ancient shantung suit up on a chair and closed his eyes, seeing nothing now but the corn-colored down on Alba's sinewy arm. The wolves still went on howling, far, far away. They must be marking out new territory, urinating on warm stones, sand, and tree trunks stripped of their bark. They must be hunting down other horses, stags, and hinds, before going back to the underground lairs that their mates had dug among the trees. Here each male supplied food for a litter of up to eight offspring, until the cubs were two years old. What a sense of responsibility!

There was murder in the air, an atmosphere of orgy. Not the passion-quelling orgy of debauch, but the orgy of rape, generating longing for death.

The Old Man's room, in this so-called luxury hotel, was full of decaying or mummified cockroaches, he wasn't sure which. He tried to sleep, to escape from the whinnying of the horse, the fingers of the violinist, Alba's arms, Vespasian's rasping voice, the barman and his Billie—on the sunny side of the world. To sleep, to escape from the yearning one sometimes has to annihilate everything, not in order to wrest its secret from the surrounding conspiracy of silence but, on the contrary, in order to *lend* it some mystery.

What are our visions made of? The Old Man, in a kind of half-waking state at once lucid and yet uncontrolled enough to be disturbing, could see how his visions were formed—the artifice behind them, and why they were so upsetting.

Of course they were false, or rather factitious—at any rate they always added something to or subtracted something from the reality they inevitably missed. This was what made them seem more real than reality itself, just as, detached from their usual context, they appeared more intense. But such images are unstable because of the music they make with our drives. Nightmare lies somewhere between sight and the inner sense of hearing. Unpronounceable words beat a rhythm for something, not yet an idea, that merely vibrates with pleasure or horror. Then, without any perceptible transition, it joins with a glimpse of a face, a scene, an animal, a plant, or some other object, some being or nonbeing. The impact of this makes the visible image break up, overflow, twist, stretch, lengthen, shrink, expand, founder, wax, wane, thin out: the resulting apparition is a kind of monster . . .

The shapes unfolding before the Old Man's eyes—exaggerated, exfoliated, eccentric, exiled, exorbitant, exceptional, excited, exciting—reproduced things he had seen the day before. But they also, in their hostile and amorphous mass, reflected the fear that ravaged him, and his inability to fight evil otherwise than by transforming it into something within himself—an inner grimace, a scrawl of images, some kind of attack, a crystal of rage, a swollen spleen, a perforated ulcer. And these silent writhings, these wordless ghosts of a wound—were *they* objective or subjective? He really didn't know any more, lying there between the sheets of that rustic bed in the lime-tinged moonlight.

But the ogres who terrify us on the screen of our dreams can also purge us of fear. An image may relax the stomach muscles, a vision may soothe pain. Acting as a guardian of sleep, it dismantles the barrier of forms and swallows up the whole body until it is unconscious of evil and thus unconscious of everything. Such is the opaque peace of sleeping sufferers.

But visible matter was starting to throb again, to weave its monsters once more. "My parents have disappeared." "You all look as though you're running away." "Wolves never panic." "It all depends on how you look at it." "The future looks decidedly bleak." Alba's and Vespasian's words echoed and took on form inside his skull.

A frozen plain; the face of someone who might have been a man if his ears hadn't been so hairy and his eyes so phosphorescent. He was chasing a beggar woman. Or perhaps she was a witch. She had a sack full of little dolls: stolen babies; infants premature and imperfect; dead fetuses, which give pain inside men as well as women. Overhead flew a carnivorous bird, its beak plunged into the heart of a creature clutched in its unrelenting talons. Its prey, its shadow.

A fantastic, incredible film. Of course no such thing could exist. "I'm dreaming," thought the Old Man, trying, but only half-heartedly, to wake up.

But it was nonetheless true that "everyone was running away," that "my parents have disappeared," that "it depended on the way you looked at it," and that "the future was bleak," if you listened to the regal voice, the falsely nonchalant disdain of Vespasian, with his mocking smile like a claw stabbing you in the lung, stopping your breath, making your ears roar with the sound of bats, your stomach burst with the aborted fetuses that witches stuff into their sacks. A frantic flight through the snow, Alba's icy solitude, a baleful little puppet, an old man's dazed fear.

What is the stuff our images are really made of, then? What is the substance they derive from, at once artificial and painful, yet so platitudinous and devoid of mystery? For once you identify the sounds and the shapes—as the Old Man did in that half-waking state, part unbearable dream, part hallucination—

no enigma remains. Monsters recover their real weight; yesterday's words throw light on the play-acting (Septicius admitted it did have an element of passion), the sham fight to the death that human beings are always inventing in order to avoid giving up the ghost there and then. The fight to the death between Alba and Vespasian, between the Old Man and the wolves, between Santa Varvara and the invaders. "My parents have disappeared." "Everyone is running away." That's all. Nothing to be done. Click. Zap. Words invoke fantasies, but they explain them too. They tame and blur the images on the TV screen of our dreams, producing finally the torpor of anguish, the stupor of sickness. The Old Man groped for words, the better to flee them by generating his own monsters. For such monsters represent a desire not dead, a desire for death. And a desire for life, the disaster that goes on and on through error after error, and will go on doing so. For how long? The answer is obvious. Forever.

⚘ 3. Anamorphoses

1

A YEAR had gone by. Or two. And once more they were at the seaside in the fall, in the same resort with its moth-eaten luxury hotels. All a little older, a little harder, under the lime trees surrounding the dance floor.

There was less and less to eat. The wolves carried off everything. But the television channels were getting more with-it— you could even get foreign stations sometimes—and traveling salesmen had managed to introduce exotic products on to the black market: mauve lipstick, fish-net stockings, and weight-reducing diets based on such rare ingredients as eggs and pineapples.

Vespasian, who saw the scalpel as the only means of practicing medicine without actually having to look after people, had specialized as a surgeon. To say he shrank from looking after people was putting it mildly. In his view, caring for patients involved not only sentimentality but also—worse still— hypocrisy, inevitably fueled by morbid pity. No, thanks! Count him out! Vespasian, ruthless and brusque, considered his time too precious for that sort of thing, and as for charity—his term for caring and all that it entailed—it only made people weak by depriving them of what little power of resistance they still possessed. In any case, the half measures that masqueraded as treatment—and this included 99 percent of all pharmacology— did no more in most cases than prolong some congenital inadequacy. Applying his own absolute method—cutting out an ulcer here, replacing a piece of old heart there with a snippet of plastic or metal—he exercised the ancient art of Hippocrates oblivious of the fact that he was ever dealing with an actual man or woman. He seemed to be afflicted with that mental impatience that is a kind of excitation without discharge—the same mania that makes for constant changes in electronic equipment, which passes from new to old in the course of a few months, from superefficient to ultra-outmoded before it is even used, a sheer delight for technologists but of little if any use to people in general. Thus all Vespasian's operations were exploits of the greatest virtuosity, and his way of thinking had so prevailed in Santa Varvara that if, as was often the case, his patient happened to die, instead of blaming the surgeon everyone put the mishap down to chance or fate or the patient's "nonviability." And Vespasian's fame as a surgeon grew and grew.

As for the part of himself his profession allowed to survive, that became increasingly ferocious. Out of resentment.

At one time Vespasian had had ideas, ideals even, he said. He had fought, too, he insisted, and this seemed probable enough; but then he'd given up—he didn't know what was worth fighting for any more. Was it worth fighting to be recognized? Naturally. And to be famous and admired. But by whom? By what? By this world of wolves? How revolting! But was there any other? No? Well, then . . . Disgust made his jowls droop; his black eyes grew expressionless, as if covered by an inoperable cataract. But Vespasian couldn't allow himself to flinch. He thought it more masculine to brace himself. A spasm ran up his arm, his neck froze, his whole body split in two along his spine: the left side as stiff as if it were in plaster, the right shaken to pieces by continual tremors. No, that wasn't it, either. He gritted his teeth and his lips protruded like the beak of a vulture. The grimace made his heavy jaws seem to taper to a hook, while his eyes shrank to pinpoints like the holes in the rubber teats at which autistic infants stare in terror.

2

In moments of anguish and rage Vespasian became quite terrifying. Even when the apparently incipient convulsion passed over and his muscles relaxed, his face took on the malevolent form of his words. Alba could no longer tell what he resembled most—a hyena, a jackal, or a vulture. She would wait, petrified, for a blow, a bite, a spurt of blood or venom.

"You've made me look ridiculous again." (Vespasian to Alba, numb with fright.)

"What?" (Alba, impassive.)

"Don't be stupid—you know what I mean. Somebody at the military hospital has pointed out to me that a woman like you—a woman whose name is Alba Ram—oughtn't really to be an officer's wife." (Vespasian, martial.)

"I thought you were a doctor." (Alba, limpid.)

"I'm an army doctor—that's different. It involves responsibility, secrets, affairs of state. Things you can have no idea of—naturally. There isn't any room for a female called Ram in that sort of context. Runaways aren't the most reliable of people, you know." (Vespasian, with the vulgarity typical of big shots.)

The disappearance of Alba's parents had had a fatal effect on Vespasian's interest in her—an interest that both the principals had hitherto taken for love. But in the light of recent events it emerged that the army doctor's desire for the girl with bronze hair had been due to her family's modest prestige. However, the invasion of the wolves, the terror they inspired everywhere, together with the undermining of the traditional principles that local worthies like the Rams had stood for, had combined to quench Vespasian's rare spurts of affection. In his view, the new situation made any attempt at courtesy and decorum quite superfluous and justified his own version of the scorched-earth policy, which consisted of meeting bad with worse, without regard to good or evil. He translated his philosophy into action by shamelessly indulging his own exacting moods and uncompromising ambitions. It was a narrow enough agenda: all he wanted was to be flattered by everyone, at home and at the hospital, and to exercise undivided power. Amazing that so limited an aim could transform such an ordinary man into an animal as grotesque as anything in the Professor's nightmares. But passion is especially pernicious when taken over by its lurking element of hatred, and Vespasian had married Alba Ram just when her parents disappeared and she lost all her charm for him. Thereafter he took great pleasure in keeping up a relationship in which he played the part of the protector who tramples the victim of his charity underfoot.

"I can't do anything about it." (Alba, an ant.)

"*I* can." (Vespasian, a tank driver.)

" . . . ?" (Alba, languidly.)

"One has to choose, for heaven's sake! It's obvious!" (Vespasian, carnivorous.)

"And you'd choose your career rather than your family?" (Alba, biblical.)

"Oh, so Milady's playing the innocent now, is she? How can anyone be so idiotic! Do you really think feelings are important in this day and age? Anyone would think we're living in the Renaissance, or in the catacombs, or some such. Not in the here and now, anyway. And Milady's shocked, is she? Whatever next!" (Vespasian, imperial but in an empire already in decline.)

Alba kept telling herself she loved him, that she'd loved him once and therefore had to love his face whatever it turned into—to love all his aspects, love him absolutely. She tried to persuade herself a woman was supposed to welcome her lover's hidden faces, that she ought to let them develop freely and wear themselves out, for in this way only, by means of her patient love, he might find peace. That's what she told herself, but her skin, her physical being, couldn't agree. It shrank painfully, became dry and cold. Her stomach swelled with blood, her heart became blocked as if with a liquid that could find no issue, and her throat was a red-hot coal that burned up every word before it was spoken. Drops of tension welled up behind the silent gleam of her eyes.

"That's all we needed! And crazy as well! Don't imagine you can get around me with tears! Madame Bovary doesn't cut any ice here! Doesn't all I've done for you count for anything? Didn't I take you in after your parents died? Well, disappeared if you prefer—it comes to the same thing! Don't forget I'm the one who feeds you, who gives you status, an excuse for being here. And that's very important for a foreigner, isn't it?" (Vespasian the vulture.)

"But I don't regard myself as a foreigner. I'm *not* a foreigner." (Alba, waking up.)

"You know what it is to be Madame Vespasian, don't you? It's a great stroke of luck, that's what it is! Of course you don't realize it—nothing is good enough for Mademoiselle Ram! She always wants more, and wants the other person to feel guilty into the bargain." (Vespasian the hyena.)

" 'It is hard to say what was most shameful about his marriages: the way he entered into them, the way he ended them, or the way he kept them up.' " (Alba, scholarly.)

"Can't understand a word she says, either." (Vespasian, naive.)

"That was Suetonius, talking about Caligula." (Alba, steely.)

"Who cares? You live in your dreams. Bad dreams, what's more. Head or guts—one has to choose, my dear, and I don't care for your choice at all." (Vespasian, threatening.)

Did he mean what he said? The tongue may escape the control of thought: it can never escape the power of passion. Speech will always reflect a thought unjustly true.

3

At the beginning of conscience there was courtesy. But mustn't conscience be a sham, a mere hypocrisy, if drink can so quickly destroy it? Vespasian would come home wild-eyed, perspiring, unsteady on his feet, unable to control himself or anything else. His glass, his knife, the jug of water on the table—any one of them might suddenly crash to the floor. It was all because of the wolves, Alba was sure. On top of everything else, when he didn't actually bury himself in silence he would babble ceaselessly, with words that were precise enough, but garrulous and spiteful. He enjoyed caricaturing Alba's gestures, her posture, her provincial accent. He was right, of course: other people's mannerisms are terribly irritating—why hadn't she thought of it before? The discovery made her withdraw behind a forbidding exterior.

Sometimes, having asked her to dine out in some restaurant, he would say at the end of the evening, "I suppose I have to pay, as usual?" She would protest: "No! I can afford it now! I'm not so badly off now as when my parents died." And she'd get out her check-book. "Certainly not!" he'd say then. "Of course I'll pay—I'm your husband, aren't I?"

"The only thing he has in common with his namesake, the Divine Vespasian, is greed," Alba would tell the Old Man, embarrassed at her own indiscretion. But at the same time she was relieved, for the Professor was the only one who could understand such a secret. Scholasticus had taught his students not to underestimate the minor characteristics of great men— it was one way of debunking authority. "It was you who taught me that Vespasian's son Titus criticized him for contemplating a tax on urine," said the young Latinist. The Professor noted with pleasure such timid vestiges of resistance: the bride, though still docile, was lucid.

Vespasian, having paid the bill for dinner, would drive home in a highly dangerous manner, either to throw a scare into Alba or because he was drunk. "Both, more like," she thought. And shrank back even further behind that waxenly impassive mask.

4

Alba cooked as some people make love: skillfully but with indifference, her mind on the pleasure of others. By so doing she would occasionally experience some pleasure herself.

Anyhow, what else was there to do, now that the teaching of Latin had been abolished in the schools and she was out of a job? Translation? Publishing? She might just as well try to confront the wolves. Cooking was one of the few remaining alternatives—the natural art of those who are naturally made use of and forgotten.

Hence her famous shoulder of pork cooked with fifty cloves. She absolutely must make it that very day: trivial distractions may become more necessary than artificial respiration. Alba hurried to the butcher's. The store never looked quite clean, but it had everything. She spent a long time selecting her particular shoulder: it had to be nice and plump, fresh, pink next to the bone, and properly trimmed of fat. All the shoulders of pork looked the same, really, but Alba did her best to find or invent details to draw out her decision, thus proving herself a "real connoisseur" to the butcher and a pain in the neck to his wife.

But Alba's purchase was the first step in a kind of alchemy, a process that induced a curious combination of exaltation and insensibility—one of the main virtues of such domestic occupations.

First the meat had to be put to soak overnight in warm water, together with ten onions cut in four. (Why four?). Next morning came the decisive phase, which spiced the officiant's calm with a tinge of anxiety: the meat had to be simmered for two and a half hours in water that must on no account be allowed to boil. The pork must stay tender—must emerge neither raw nor cooked. A very tricky and challenging business! While the meat was draining you prepared the sauce—the high point of the whole magic operation. You melted some butter and brown sugar—*never* white, of course—and added some of the liquid in which the meat had soaked, plus some cayenne pepper and a few slices of pineapple (this from Alba's varied stock of canned foods). The quantities depended on your mood: taste is an unpredictable female whim. By now it was time to stick your fifty cloves into the shoulder of pork and put it in the oven to turn brown and pink and gold. The dénouement was as confused as the birth of a baby: the infant emerged from the oven ready to satisfy all appetites, while the mother disappeared behind a weary smile, prepared for every kind of disappointment.

Vespasian ate with brutish greed, crouching over his plate and emitting indecipherable growls by way of compliment. Alba ate nothing. The steam, the smells, the sensations of the cooking had been enough for her. Now she could tell herself Vespasian loved her after all. And hide away in her kitchen to escape the wolves. To every man his own lair. People find what refuge they can.

5

"All quite dreadful but quite ordinary," was the Old Man's diagnosis. He saw everything, but went on pondering over his *Meadows*, the inexpressible *Prata* of his fragmented thought, the novel that disintegrated through impatience before anything solid could happen.

When something is ordinary it is nondescript, devoid of all specificity: an empty shell, a dim hideout, a timorous den, a carapace, a crust, a vestige, a bit of debris.

No dents, no protuberances, nothing exceptional or individual left. Trivial shocks are too small and obvious to make any impact. The obvious is what has lost its meaning but still reflects the primal, minimal conditions of the human animal: eating, drinking, defecating, attacking, defending itself, sleeping, being afraid or angry or ashamed, feeling pleasure or displeasure. The ordinary is the protoplasm of our lives, which make a miserly pact with ungratified desire. The ordinary soaks up fervor, acrimony, torpor, deceit, error, horror, happiness, stupor, the passing hour. It swallows our humble attempts at originality, grinds up our follies with an implacable "That's life," which makes any disturbance seem dull. It swallows up word play and wit—those seemingly modest enemies of the ordinary that are really the only ones that last—and turns them into childishness. The ordinary is always right: it turns us into undifferentiated copies, dreary duplicates of our biological destinies, inarticulate masses of organs.

It is the lowest form of human arrangement. Tedious, too: no sooner have you settled, reassured and drowsy, into banality, than you're weary of it, as the Old Man knew all too well. Then the desire for something to happen, the longing for surprise, breaks the pact and smashes the incubator ceaselessly reproducing the ravenous ovaries and fleeting spermatozoa of your loves and hates. Something, anything, has got to happen: birth or death, sight or flight. Let there be something unusual, strange, peculiar! Shatter this order, show me the extraordinary! The ecstatic, the rapturous, the out-of-the-way, the outlandish, the outlawed! But is it possible? The ordinary is still there, on the alert, ready to blunt the point of your eccentricities. And events—which can never equal their sacred prototypes, birth and death—are swiftly drowned in the ruthless depths of "That's life."

So there's no solution? Yes, there probably is a way out. Try! the Professor would say sardonically. Keep on holding aloof. Persist against the ordinary. Mistrust arrangement. Confront the permanence of compromise with the constancy of refusal. Exaggerate! Persevere! If you're talkative, awkward, raving, avid, or delinquent; an eater, a drinker or a smoker; a vagabond or a visionary; an artist or an anchorite; slanderer or slandered—if you're any of these, fight the good fight against the ordinary, don't miss any chances, the odds are against you! But be sure not to nourish any hope. On the basis of your ordinary despair, that weak yet enduring foundation, rise up continually, all of you, against the pact of domestication! Disunite against the ordinary!

You don't have the physical strength, the verbal vigor, the useful insomnia that support the unusual ones, the fortunate loners? No? Then you're reduced to Alba and Vespasian's solution: playing at the ordinary together. Taking an interest in uninteresting misfortunes, paltry setbacks that enliven your relationships—pale, flabby, viscous, malevolent, pathetic relationships that they are, but so nourishing, warming, snug, numbing, almost beautiful. Wolves are said to lick their own wounds, gnawing at them, curing them so as to be able to make others in their place. True or false? In the same way, you can keep stoking up your special little perversity (a poor thing but your own)—the ordinary is satisfied with little, with nothing, with anything. You can go on eating one another mentally, morally, sensually, sexually, metaphysically, and physically until you're wretched, confused, stupid, wicked, unhappy enough to die of shame, rage, or pleasure. You may even resort to murder. But it isn't really murder, because it's so obvious and inevitable: there's no way out, that's life, it's absolutely domestic, domestically absolute, the inexorable platitude of nondescript passion, the horribly bearable ordinariness of death.

At the point of ordinariness where human beings fall into decline—or, worse still, into insignificance—a certain inertia incorporates us into the new community of wolves. Of innocuous wolves. Does such a deterioration worry you? Does it even horrify you? You don't say! But you know perfectly well, just as well as the Old Man, what's left of great plans and bright ideals. So isn't it simpler and more ordinary (I grant you that) to opt for crazy indifference, for innocent folly?

It was easy to imagine Alba and Vespasian talking like that, but difficult—unless one were Ovid or Goya, or the elderly dreamer who put himself in the place of artists dead and gone—to see who could shake such people out of their indigence.

Lousy old ordinariness. A permanent waste product of the everyday, of which people are ashamed though at the same time they secretly enjoy it. But is it as secretly as all that? The secrecy of the ordinary is a kind of psychological dirt: the psychological as unconscious excretion. Soil your neighbor as you soil yourself; don't fight; don't have aspirations; don't breathe; shrink, be sly, be vengeful, wear a mask, be realistic—you know what illusions lead to.

But is savagery really any more harmless when it's ordinary? "There's no solution," thought the Old Man. But he went on pursuing his visions. Septicius Clarus was no ordinary pessimist.

6

Women's hatred curls up inside them like a uterus. It's there beyond the vagina, unthought-of but unctuous, not necessarily painful nor even perceptible, always rather distant and hidden, as if belonging to another world. Shifty, you might say. But that's not really it. Detached, rather. It belongs to a category of its own; it exists in some remote compartment of an inaccessible nonconsciousness. It's a hatred that's physical, opaque, intransigent, but not overt, not accounted for in the ordinary ledger of days and nights.

Sometimes this uterine hatred is unconscious: it may be disguised as patience, or love, or—more frequently—a resigned and indulgent lethargy. For women, despite moments of rebellion, which instead of freeing them merely increase their subjection, are bound to be faithful to the influence of their mothers: so they always manage to get hold of someone they hope will one day come through but who always fails lamentably to do so.

This someone, whether a child or a man, is your burden; you asked for it. He surprises you, disappoints you, hurts you; he will puzzle you, he will puzzle himself—who can say? But, for now, there's nothing to be done but give in and say nothing. It's called loving. Or hating.

The more Alba shriveled up in her thwarted loathing, the more like a medlar she looked. No fruit is more unattractive: it's a kind of lusterless, shapeless, brownish-yellow lump. Even Alba's auburn hair, perched on the top of her head in a bun, looked washed-out and lank: she had the monastic gloom of a restive bay mare. But inside its skin the medlar is soft and velvety, bland and soothing. It's not like chocolate; it's neither sweet nor sour; it's something in between, something that tastes like transition itself. For Alba, hatred was a lifeline that in some incomprehensible fashion bridged a gap and made her whole, saving her from the terrifying void into which she was hurled by Vespasian's stinging words. A wolf and a medlar don't go together; nothing could be more pointless and ridiculous than a marriage between them. Did Vespasian have any idea of the vegetable hatred that existed so near him? In the rare moments when sobriety replaced the animal fury that now did duty as his nervous system, he was capable of imagining the latent resentment harbored by his Alba, wrapped up in her medlar skin and secretly sipping the nourishing juice of contempt. Contempt for him, Vespasian. And the wolf sometimes thought that maybe the medlar was right.

When his metamorphoses were only just beginning, Vespasian still desired Alba. He would make love to her with furious pleasure, and ask her to tell him stories about rape. Surely someone must have raped her some time? She was certainly worth it. When? Where? Was the rapist good at it? What was his erection like? But perhaps there were others besides him? Did he beat her up? Did *they* beat her up? Alba blushed, the medlar started to shrink: instead of sweet flesh it contained only the bitter dryness that precedes disgust. But a woman is made like a nest of Russian dolls: you can always extract another one and make it talk. In the role of whom or what? Of nothing, of course, for all that's there is a series of dolls with an empty hole in the middle. So the shriveled medlar would invent a tale of rape to arouse the wolf, the jackal, the vulture.

But the animal got bored. Had he seen through her stratagem, or was he finally paralyzed by his own rage? Whatever the explanation, he lost interest. Desire, even at its most brutish, is a kind of frantic sweetness. But Vespasian was no longer either frantic or tender. All that was left was the writhing of cells and words that seek only to hurt because they can't be bothered with anything internal. For Alba, on the other hand, the body was inhabited by a mind teeming with images. But her imperial husband claimed he possessed neither the one nor the other.

A pervert, like a lover, selects an idol or at least a fetish to adore. But Vespasian had no inner shrine at which to worship: he had fenced it round with frontiers, and inhabited an area with reversible borders and merely temporary thresholds. He was ready to do anything, and thus was indifferent to everything. That didn't stop him from being implacable.

Strangely enough, people lose both their form and their content when they live on a watershed between two eras. Lacking both inside and outside, they either indulge in violent deeds and explode, or wither into a mineral state of meaningless impenetrability. The choice is between active monsters and monstrous insignificance.

Alba liked to contemplate Vespasian's cancerous protuberances, the sarcomas of what, according to the Professor, "had once been the soul." She didn't realize that a feeling witness of such metamorphoses is necessarily contaminated.

So it would be wrong to think women's anger is limited to uterine viscosity. A medlar can easily turn into a Hecuba. True, Alba had no son to avenge. But even humility may grow exhausted, and make bone itself shriek beneath its bloody hand. "While he spoke and forswore himself, she listened with a wild look, and anger boiled up in her and brimmed over. Her anger gave her strength. She drove her fingers into the traitor's eyes and tore the orbs from their cavities, plunging her hands into the villain's blood and scouring not the eyes, for they had gone, but the orbits." No one could ever have approved of such a revenge. Even her old Scholasticus, who had taught her that passage from Ovid, would have rained arrows and stones on her if he'd so much as suspected she was capable of it. "But she, with a hoarse groan, pursued and tried to bite the piece of rock that had been thrown at her, and instead of the words she tried to say there came from her open mouth the barking of a dog." A bitch. The place where it happened is still there. Anyone can see "the bitch's tomb" on the Hellespont, near Abydos.

"*At haec missum rauco cum murmure saxum / Morsibus insequitur rictuque in verba parato / latravit, conata loqui;*

locus extat et ex re / Nomen habet veterumque diu memor illa malorum / Tum quoque Sithonios uluavit maesta per agros." What genius! *"Illius Troasque suos hostesque Pelasgos, / Illius fortuna deos quoque moverat omnes, / Sic omnes, ut et ipsa Iovis coniunxque sororque / Eventus Hecubam meruisse negaverit illos."* "His misfortune moved his subjects the Trojans, his enemies the Pelasgians, and even all the gods . . . "

Of course, Hecuba was only a fantasy: a civilized woman would never do such a thing. Alba watched Ovid's tale unfold, and only her medlar flesh kept her inside her brown and now unprepossessing skin (for holding back one's hate makes one ugly), prevented her from digging her sharp nails into the eye, or rather the face of her attacker. That face was unrecognizable to her now, reduced to a pool of mud by an anger that had once been desire but of which nothing now remained. Nothing.

Murder. It was bound to end in murder. The Old Man didn't like to think about it, but he feared it more and more. It was obvious. And what is obvious is what is almost bound to happen when you're afraid.

7

Another stormy night filled Septicius's room with new nightmares, in which Alba and Vespasian mingled with monsters, wolves, and Hecubas.

Scraps of ancient poetry, bits of forgotten paintings, the full moon piercing through shutters and eyelids—all combined to make up a terrifying montage that was somehow more real than what he'd seen of his young friends the previous evening, when they were all together again in the run-down luxury hotel by the sea.

The moonlight, glancing off the lime trees around the dance floor, pried into the dark bedroom and irradiated the monstrous images without placating them.

A vulture with a wolf's head was devouring the breast of a woman lying stretched out on the ground.

Naked bodies were heaped up in pyramids, with cats' faces in the place of their private parts.

Lecherous asses let themselves be ridden by frenzied men with heads like birds of prey.

The Old Man felt the wall move and bend over his bed. He had to get up and ward it off with all the strength of his arms and chest and thighs. As he did so he was surrounded by simian faces.

This dream was driven off by the banging of a window in a sudden gust of wind, but the nightmare wasn't over.

A dying man was writing "Nothing" on a notepad, and the old man, recognizing himself, felt better for a while. The monsters were rejecting the best blessing of existence—its nothingness. Ovid might have understood that "Nothing." For if there are too many metamorphoses they cancel one another out, though they do not disappear. Thus, once the weird and wonderful shapes that went on incurring the wrath of Rome had been poured out, the poet, banished by Augustus, found peace beside the Black Sea.

But it was only a respite. The gust of wind was just the prelude to a storm. Rain whipped the concrete dance floor, where a dwarf was staggering about, smiling horribly and stretching out a grotesquely enormous hand toward the sleeper's face.

And the wolf with the changing face appeared again, wrapped in a shawl, surrounded by black men, bats, and witches, and writing down some morbid maxim or other.

It was the thunder that finally woke Septicius up.

"Was it Ovid or Goya?" The Old Man tried to smile. He didn't like to ring for the barman to bring him his tea. "Is it still night, or morning?" A sluggish gray curtain veiled the coastline, lashed by the tropical storms of late summer. "I'm getting gloomier as I get older. But is age ever an excuse? A man is as old as his dreams."

This notion amused the Old Man. He drank his tea, for it was eight o'clock by now and the barman had just brought it in as usual. There was a twig of lime on the tray, in honor of their shared admiration for Billie Holliday.

The Old Man's nightmares now threw a new light on certain important matters. Confused lyricism over, the silence that follows throws out what is intolerable.

He must find Alba and her martial husband. He was worried by their behavior. By the imminence of murder. The wolves were at it again.

8

"The beach is polluted and the women are hideous: graceless lumps of flesh." (Vespasian.)

"I saw a gull swoop down to catch a fish. So cruel and precise. Beautiful." (Alba.)

"All you think about is birds and yourself. It's impossible to have a proper conversation with you." (Vespasian.)

"It was full moon last night." (Alba.)

"You see!" (Vespasian.)

Alba was silent.

"There's a rave review in the *Santa Varvara Courier* about the soap opera that was on last night. But as you never watch television it won't mean anything to you . . . By the way, it's been announced that the cost of living has gone up again. Army pay will follow, of course."

"Is that in the *Courier* too?" (Alba.)

"Of course not! Don't be silly! But you ought to be glad—it affects you, doesn't it? Because it affects me!" (Vespasian.)

"People are turning into wolves. It was bound to happen." (Alba.)

"There you go again! But it's only natural—the price we have to pay for progress." (Vespasian.)

"We ought to sleep, and show each other a lot of affection." (Alba.)

"That's right! You'll always be a child. A gloomy child." (Vespasian.)

"We mustn't give in." (Alba.)

"What to?" (Vespasian.)

"Boredom. Giving in comes from boredom." (Alba.)

"There are worse things." (Vespasian.)

"Yes. Images. Instead of wondering 'What will people say? '—our parents' watchword, though people have begun to laugh at it now—we have a craze for creating an image of ourselves. A one-day wonder in the papers or on television." (Alba.)

"Not many manage to achieve it." (Vespasian.)

"Quite. Think of all the competition!" (Alba.)

"But images like that are meaningless. People who want them are dummies." (Vespasian.)

"The choice is between wolves and dummies. Sometimes they're one and the same." (Alba.)

"Sometimes." (Vespasian.)

"More and more often. You want an image too. I know." (Alba.)

"I can do without. It's not my job. But showbiz isn't a crime." (Vespasian.)

"I don't know. Maybe it's a perversion? Nothing's forbidden, and yet everything is. Nothing's written down, everything passes." (Alba.)

"Why not? Life must take its course." (Vespasian.)

"The Professor's still alive." (Alba.)

"Some life! He's just a relic. A sleepwalker." (Vespasian.)

"He's a standard. A counterweight. What's become of culture? I love him." (Alba.)

"I don't." (Vespasian.)

"You're too . . . " (Alba.)

"Too what? I'm waiting." (Vespasian.)

"Too animal." (Alba.)

"Do you mean too erotic?" (Vespasian.)

"That's a matter of taste." (Alba.)

"Don't I appeal to you any more?" (Vespasian.)

"Yes . . . But I only see you for a couple of hours a day, including meals." (Alba.)

"Work!" (Vespasian.)

"Power." (Alba.)

"Exactly!" (Vespasian.)

"So what about boredom?" (Alba.)

"What is it?" (Vespasian.)

"It's when the word *together* becomes unthinkable." (Alba.)

"Worse things happen." (Vespasian.)

"Hatred." (Alba.)

"Let's not exaggerate." (Vespasian.)

"Don't tell me you don't know what it is!" (Alba.)

"We live in a changing world." (Vespasian.)

"A world eager for profit, but a world that's lazy too. The search for pleasure at any price can only produce monsters." (Alba.)

"Monsters? Who says so?" (Vespasian.)

"Ovid." (Alba.)

"No! Ovid thought metamorphoses were quite natural." (Vespasian.)

"Only in a way. They could be undesirable. A kind of degeneration." (Alba.)

"How sanctimonious! But one can't make even bad literature out of noble sentiments these days." (Vespasian.)

"I *am* sentimental. Or rather I was." (Alba.)

"How tedious! But I could have told you what would happen." (Vespasian.)

9

She was amazed they were still at one in their disharmony. He thought no other woman had auburn hair like hers, and that it made up for her medlarlike intensity.

The Old Man came over to them, holding a glass of orange juice in his hand. The barman stood behind the counter as if aware he was an interloper, waiting for the moment when he could get drunk again on the dark voice of his idol.

"May I join you? . . . You've forgotten all about Tibullus, my dears!" (Septicius Clarus.)

"Who?" (Vespasian.)

"And again—forgive me for dreaming in broad daylight: '*O quantum est auri pereat potiusque smaragdi, / Quam fleat ob nostras ulla puella vias.*' 'I'd sooner all the gold in the world should vanish, together with all the emeralds, rather than that my travels should make one girl whom I love shed tears.' '*Non ego laudari curo, mea Delia: tecum / Dum modo sim, quaeso segnis inersque vocer; / Te spectem, suprema mihi cum venerit hora, / Te teneam moriens deficiente manu.*' 'No, I don't trouble myself about glory, my Delia: I don't mind being called lazy and a coward, if only I may be with you, may look at you when my hour comes, and touch you with my faltering hand as I die!' Do you follow? How wonderfully delicate, isn't it?" (The Old Man.)

"And yet, after his *discidium* with Delia, he took Marathus as a lover, and then he had that violent passion for Nemesis, the imaginary courtesan . . . " (Alba, the loyal but skeptical pupil.)

"No doubt, no doubt, but what an exquisite soul that young man had—lights and shadows perfectly balanced. And yet he died before Christ, a long time before Plotinus. Just think—a Roman who eschewed fame, and apparently shunned war and orgies too."

"I prefer 'Nights full of passion, jealousy, and hate.' " (The Barman, impatient.)

"You're a dreamer, Professor, a latter-day romantic, and in love with Delia . . . Sorry, with Alba." (Vespasian.)

"No doubt, no doubt, young man. Eros, Amor. *'Parcite, quam custodit Amor, violare puellam / Ne pigeat magno post didicisse malo.'*

'Do not profane a girl who is watched over by Love, lest later, through terrible chastisement, you learn that she is so protected.' There used to be links between people then, and yet they weren't bound. Freedom—neither passion nor indifference—is a link, perhaps. Then it was our turn, the turn of the Christians, and the turn of what's left of them in Santa Varvara. I'm one of them, of course . . . But what's become of Ovid and Tibullus?—and even Suetonius, Alba, if you insist? For that's the question, isn't it? What has become of them?" (The Old Man.)

"Disappeared. It goes without saying." (Vespasian.)

"That's just a hypothesis, young man, a mere hypothesis. *I* think they've undergone a metamorphosis. Into what? Into us. Into you. Into the barman's records. And into Santa Varvara itself—why not? And so we can find them again if we look hard enough. In the original texts, of course; in the ruins of ancient palaces and churches; and even in the thoughts of people whose faces alter. Have you noticed?—their faces change into the faces of wolves, don't they? Don't tell me you haven't seen them all around you. But there are still traces of their old selves in them, in you . . . '*It's foolish but it's fun.*' We mustn't be afraid of the wolves. I myself keep looking for signs of my friends from the old days." (The Old Man.)

"No law against deluding oneself." (Vespasian.)

"You're affected by the difference between before and after . . . Disappointed, I expect." (Alba to the Old Man, with a surreptitious glance at Vespasian.)

"In a way, in a way . . . But I stick to my guns. 'And you will weep for me, Delia, when I'm lying on the pyre about to be lit'— *Flebis et arsuro positum me, Delia, lecto, / Tristibus et lacrimis oscula mixta dabis*—'mixed with bitter tears, you will give me your kisses: your heart is not harshly bound with iron, your tender bosom doesn't contain a stone.' " (The Old Man.)

"He was obsessed. Obsessed with death." (Vespasian.)

"The opposite of a murderer." (The Old Man.)

"The people here think of nothing but dominating and killing one another." (Alba.)

"You're imagining things, darling. All they do is watch TV. What about a walk on the beach?" (Vespasian.)

The Old Man was sure this Vespasian didn't need Alba to provide him with such notions: the idea of people dominating and killing one another as they all stared in the same direction, pretending to be interested in images, comic strips, films, and television. For in Santa Varvara the beams of people's eyes never met except in a screen, which thus took the place of infinity in the old geometry . . . He was a hard man, this Vespasian, a real Lycaon. Lycaon was another character in Ovid, an enemy of Jupiter—nothing like Tibullus! Poor Alba, she'd either leave him or grow to be like him. But what could *he* do? Nothing? Still, he couldn't help worrying.

" 'Soon death will come, its head shrouded in shadow, and soon will come numbing age . . . ' One day—is it so far off as you think, my children?—your language will be as dead as the Latin I try to bring to life again. So make the most of it, make the most of it. *'Interea, dum fata sinunt, iungamus amores: / Iam, venit tenebris Mors adoperta caput.'* 'So long as the fates permit, let us love one another. Soon death will come, its head shrouded in darkness.' (The Professor, walking away.)

"Poetry is his charm." (Alba.)

"The charm of the weak."(Vespasian.)

"You frighten me," Alba thought, though she didn't say anything. Fear made her look serious and therefore beautiful; but miserable too. They disappeared into the breeze blowing through the lime trees. Beyond stretched out the white expanse of sand.

Part Two

DETECTIVE STORY

⁓ 4. Neither More nor Less

1

THAT'S HOW the tale of the Old Man and the wolves might begin, as seen from a distance by a hidden, anonymous observer, the author in disguise. But if the master of ceremonies should reveal himself and include himself in the story, then the narrative, whether dreamlike so far or literary, plausible or grotesque, is ipso facto transformed into a quest after mysteries, a police inquiry. And the form of the narrative, the twists and turns of the plot, the changes of genre, will depend on choices made by the narrator himself in terms of space, distance, and psychological geometry.

You're invited into a new and outlandish world inhabited by strange characters, fossils of an unknowable, apparently dead civilization, unapproachable monsters speaking a dead or even nonexistent language. This angle of vision invests the writer with a neutrality that is a kind of arrogance: the presumptuousness of those who are sure of themselves and of traditions and beliefs that conceal a tendency to jump to conclusions. In other words, a fundamental stupidity. But it's a much-esteemed stupidity, thought to be noble and creative, which establishes the writer's authority without troubling to ask how it is that this particular man and his pen have come to engender and take pleasure in these dubious creatures, these citizens of some submerged Atlantis suddenly conjured to the surface by a whim of the imagination.

But should the distant, anonymous author be struck by the oddity of all this, he is forced to call his own role into question. He instructs himself to examine his links—he soon suspects they have something to do with his own family relationships—with the strange phantoms who inhabit his pages, and who reveal to him, as if in a nightmare, incidents, either experienced or merely dreaded, from his own biography. Then he embarks on the inquiry proper, setting himself up as either policeman or archaeologist. All such investigations, from *The Purloined Letter* to *Salammbô*, have been inspired by the same kind of curiosity, and all are certain to detect some more or less sordid passion lurking beneath appearances and clues. Think of the taste of red currants, in Proust, and how the memory of a whip in a brothel returns just as the calm cathedral of *Le Temps retrouvé* is culminating in music.

Once the different parts of his ego have been split up among the characters in the thriller that has replaced his original epic, the investigator, the detective, may turn out to be quite a chameleon. He may be affectionate and lyrical, like Sherlock Holmes, James Bond, and even Mike Hammer; he may be infantilism incarnate in a bowler hat, leather boots, and a bullet-proof waistcoat, with a revolver that never misses and the last word in Batmobiles. The erstwhile contemplative researcher may be metamorphosed into a poet. The novel breaks down into fragments, into poetic prose, the occasional dash of sentiment or compassion heralding the eternal return of lucidity. And when speech reaches the extreme of its own strength and certainty, it may revert to the weakness, flexibility, and repetitiveness of its point of departure in baby talk, nursery rhymes, and lullabies. It does so not for pleasure, nor for long, but in order to bring sensation into literature, to import lyricism, which is an admission of guilt or incompleteness, into the very structure of the plot. But storytelling also relies on pleasure, the kinetic pleasure everyone feels in following a sequence of events.

So it's good to tell stories. Of course, people who are lucky enough to speak and write well as children do their best, when older and wiser, to produce taut, well-constructed tales: it's another version of contemplation, an algebraic form of orison, logic transformed into prayer. Then the novel opens out into philosophy, and the interfusion of one with the other abolishes the frontiers once drawn up between the different genres for the benefit of lazy schoolboys.

But let us also consider people who are immature, whose intelligence, developing as they—allegedly—grow up, is devoted to observing their own weaknesses: anxiety, fear, sleeplessness, stupidity, bestiality, brutality, crime . . . And who knows what else? And would I say if I knew? When people like this pluck up the courage to speak they tell stories. But while their kind of story puts the pieces together, instead of arriving at a completed jigsaw puzzle it produces only a riddle. There's a meaning here, it says, but it's a hidden meaning. There's a purpose, but its object escapes me. There's action, but who will notice and be affected by it?

The story, which tells us the little that actually happens, is simply the stage machinery behind the performance, the string that moves the puppet. If I change the way I tell my tale, the meaning of the shadows you identify with changes too, as do the proportions they contain of artifice and plausibility. The Old Man is no longer merely the Old Man; Alba may be you; and as for Vespasian . . . Who is to know who's in charge in Santa Varvara once I start interfering!

Our goings hence and our comings hither all take place in the form of stories. And, since you were born to die, the words most suitable for those two unavoidable extremes, as for all that happens in between, is a story made and unmade at the same time as what you believe to be "yourself." Beneath all the rigor of method, concept, doubt, and wager, I claim and proclaim the minor dignity, and the therapeutic, aesthetic, philosophical, even physical value of the polytopical space in which the simple-minded meet, recognize one another, and merge. The kind of people who, when they try to put into words adventures they have secreted away in order to make life bearable, dare, like me, to say "I" in lots of different ways.

2

As soon as I arrived in Santa Varvara—either through absentmindedness or perhaps because I wanted to keep you in suspense, I haven't yet made it clear that the Old Man, Alba, and Vespasian, when they weren't away on vacation, lived in the city of Santa Varvara—it seemed to me the place was haunted. I couldn't say what it was that made me think so. You've probably had the same feeling yourself, arriving at the railway station or the airport in some town that is quite new to you, but that as soon as you get there suggests sinister machinations that seem at once familiar and forgotten—unthinkable, absurd, and yet present in forms that are disturbingly real. Was it the cruel yet evasive faces of the inhabitants, who, according to what the Old Man told me later, were then in the process of being transmogrified into wolves? Was it all the death notices plastered up on walls and trees like election posters or advertisements for local dances, but lauding the virtues of the deceased so emphatically I began to wonder if the dear departed were not the victims of the necrophiliac authors, the predestined prey of morbid poets? Or was my uneasiness really the result of childhood memories? For I had spent some years in this place, and all that remained, together with a few friendships, were some of the vague stories that adolescents transform into hallucinations.

But to tell the truth I could adduce no rational basis for what I felt. It was just an impression, a sense that some crime was imminent; something I might have called anxiety if I'd been at all neurotic. As I wasn't, I just made my way in a fairly relaxed manner through Santa Varvara.

The town center was full of relics dating from the beginning of the Christian era, together with a group of ancient churches that the tourist brochures described as "unique in the whole world." The local authorities spent a lot of time restoring these edifices, converting them into museums, and generally opening or shutting them in accordance with the politics prevailing at the time. At present these ecclesiastical curiosities were deserted by their congregations. The current government had appointed false priests, and these the Old Man harassed in and out of season. "Be off!" he'd cry. "I can't bear to see a man turning religion into a profession. His face is false, he's as cold and dead as his gods." The Professor even told me that, on nights when the moon was full, the men supposed to be guarding the churches used, through "negligence," to let the wolves in.

The old town center was made up of a few Renaissance palaces and some private mansions dating from the seventeenth century. These had been requisitioned and turned into government ministries, while a number of old burghers' houses, built in no particular style and now dilapidated, were inhabited by descendants of the town's oldest families. The Old Man was one of these. To a visitor the whole area, so precarious-looking and threatened, seemed somehow rather touching. It was bordered on the south-east by a large park with a lake, where in his youth, long before the coming of the wolves, the Old Man used to like to take his daughters rowing on a Sunday, while their mother cooked the roast mutton and apple tart. But not many people went to the park now. "It's not really safe," the citizens would say, turning their cruel faces hastily away and making for the suburbs.

Santa Varvara had grown enormously in the last forty years: housing projects, apartment blocks, supermarkets, parking lots, and motorways had spread out all around it as far as the eye could see. There was an immense expanse of ever-increasing suburb: people were as anxious to get away from the fields as from the city. ("It's only natural," the Old Man told me. "The wolves can operate more easily in the country.") Santa Varvara had grown so gigantic it almost merged into Santa Domenica, which used to be a whole day's journey away. Santa Domenica itself now merged into Burgos and other small towns and villages on the coast that had turned into seaside resorts. The whole country, indeed, had become one continuous Santa Varvara, with just a few empty stretches traversed by motorways and wolves.

Alba and Vespasian lived on the twentieth floor of a high-rise building in the vast modern quarter not far from the old town center. They considered themselves quite privileged because an ultramodern fountain had just been built at the foot of their building—the last word in figurative art. It was a source of great glee to the children, and of wonder and perplexity to the old men who spent all day sitting on the benches around it. The masterpiece consisted of a pool, in the middle of which a colored sculpture depicted the disjointed limbs of a being that amongst us Lilliputians might have passed for Gulliver's wife: a giant eye, an enormous nose, red lips revealing teeth as white and shiny and massive as a kitchen sink, silicone-swollen breasts, and a nymphlike rear that could have made mincemeat of Mont Blanc at one blow, not to mention the beautiful ogress's Titanic straw hat and matching sunshade. These impressive elements all rotated around their axis with a spiral vibration that threw up great spurts of spray. The wind sometimes caught hold of these geysers and deposited them on the bystanders, much to their delight.

"Funny idea of a fountain." (Alba, risking her little-girl voice.) "Though I admit not everybody has one under their window."

"We're in the very heart of the capital!" (Vespasian, exultant.) " And what is a center? The future! . . . I ask you—have you ever seen anything better? If so, where? When? How? . . . My poor girl, you're just incapable of enthusiasm!"

The Old Man preferred to avoid the staring eye, the gigantic nose, the silicone breasts. He asked Alba to tea at his own place, in the old gray building next to the church served by false priests. And it must be admitted she accepted with alacrity, for she too felt crime lurking in Santa Varvara—creeping along the motorways, through the supermarkets and the public housing estates, and setting itself up, invisible but challenging, around the fountain and its revolving, mutilated giantess. But of course Alba was obliged to return the invitation, and then the Old Man had to haul himself up to the twentieth floor, shutting his eyes to the abhorred example of contemporary art and more worried than ever about the wolves.

They had now infiltrated everywhere.

3

The planes were on strike again, so I'd had to leave my baggage at Orly, present myself six hours later at Roissy, and then endure an interminable wait for my flight, which kept on being signaled as "delayed." In short, when I landed in Santa Varvara I hadn't had a wink of sleep for over twenty-four hours. But as soon as I'd dropped my cases off at my hotel I went straight over to see a childhood friend of mine. This was the best way to take the pulse of the country where I was raised, Papa having been ambassador there at the time. Various people must still remember my father, so his daughter Stephanie Delacour wasn't likely to be short of useful contacts. But first of all I wanted information that was concrete and direct.

Alba greeted me with the impassive expression I remembered from our days together in high school, but I realized there was something wrong even as I tried to swallow the hot but revolting coffee she'd brought me. To a perceptive eye, embarrassment was written all over her face, usually unremarkable under her helmet of dark red hair. But just now she looked beautiful. Shame was the only thing that could be lending her this distinction and giving her a personality again. "So in a way Vespasian is necessary to her," I told myself. The thought helped me fight back my repugnance at the incredibly strong brew in my cup and the racket rising up from fountain below. The mechanism of the mutilated giantess was switched on every day at sunrise.

So I heard and even partly took in the latest installment of the story Alba brought me up to date on every time I went there: a mixture of distress and relief, a kind of secret psychotherapy between friends, which helped her to stay silent until our next meeting. But of course my mind was mainly on the story I was there to write: about the political situation in Santa Varvara, vague echoes of which were heard from time to time in the world press. So, with one part of my mind on all the interviews that lay before me, I listened to my poor, pretty Alba with the preoccupied benevolence commonly attributed to psychoanalysts, though in my case it was due to a sleepless overnight journey and vague speculations about current events in Santa Varvara itself.

"Drink up your coffee, Stephie. It loses half its strength when it's cold."

She was bossy and annoying and sweet. Motherly too, and thus inevitably dreary. I made another effort to pay attention.

It seemed Vespasian regarded sex as a matter of technique. At first Alba had found him amusing. Now she'd discovered he was brutish. I wondered if she'd ever wake up to the fact that the whole thing was pathetic.

And what else?

Vespasian's laughter was noisy and ostentatious—it required no reaction, it wasn't addressed to anyone, it merely rejected whatever didn't reflect itself. Self-regarding laughter is a kind of nervous hate. Any unflattering comment bored him, except when he took it as an insult. Conversation languished, the only alternatives being ritual compliment or sulky silence.

From Alba's remarks and my own observations it was clear the marriage was on the rocks. But hatred makes people tight-lipped, and my friend, at once undermined by indignity and made more attractive by it, told her story tersely, though with determination. She doled out the trivial facts in a voice so vibrant with innuendo it made every detail portentous.

When he came home—late—he had eyes only for the television: not as a distraction but as a means of abstraction, an opportunity to be even more contemptuous of the world around him. Vespasian didn't talk any more: he was shut up inside one impermeable point of view, and shunned the human voice. Only the screen held any attraction for him: its images were bound to be fascinating because it was the powers-that-be that showed them. He looked, but did he listen? Entertainment doesn't involve a dialogue. You're either "in" or on the outside, superhuman or a nonentity, all or nothing. In any case, alone. What did Vespasian love? He loved nothing. He loved to bury himself in images that he knew to be false but that he regarded as powerful because the establishment put them on.

"You know—" (Alba kept appealing to me) "he's not conscious of leading a double life because he hasn't got a consciousness. Consciousness and unconsciousness don't apply. It's as if he was made up of a vast number of different images. A traveling exhibition of masks, each artificially constructed for an equally artificial scene. Do you think that's impossible?" (I must have been looking bored and skeptical.) "If you only knew! No, he's not ill—that's not what I mean. He's consumed with the desire to be unique wherever he goes. He lives in worlds that are all cut off from one another, and in each of which the shadows surrounding him know only one of his faces. Every place, every shadow, possesses just one, unique Vespasian. But I know all his faces—or rather all the seams that hold those tatters of faces together."

Would my friend have been so bitter if *she* had given up "holding together" her marriage? I rebuked myself for not being more supportive. But I went on listening, too sleepy to do otherwise.

4

Any phrase may be interpreted as meaning the opposite of what it actually says. A harmless or even flattering remark can become an accusation, a criticism, or a threat. "Nice day," she says. He understands her to mean, "You bore me." "Unusual and complex," she comments. "Obscure and incomprehensible" is what he hears. Is he wrong? "Suspect your wife every morning," says a universal proverb. "If you don't know why, she does." But such mistrust put Alba on the track of her own suspicion, which up till then she'd failed to recognize. At first she was surprised; then she faced up to reality. But since reality, on both sides, was simply hostility, they were both right. So what were they to do? Loathe one another or laugh? Alba and Vespasian avoided one another in order to avoid declaring war.

She didn't dare fall ill any more. This had the advantage of keeping her in rude if artificial health. For it's possible to stay well out of sheer terror. Alba did so for fear that Vespasian might explode: "This place is like a hospital! Don't you think I have enough of that at work? You should take better care of yourself!" Earlier on she'd tried to tell herself the reason he didn't want to see her laid up was that he was hypersensitive, highly strung, and loved her very much, in his own way. But now his anger didn't reassure her any more. Or arouse her, either.

If Alba actually got influenza it only made Vespasian even

less sympathetic: wasn't a wilting wife simply asking to be disliked?

"He says all in all the wolves compare favorably to the Weimar Republic." (Alba was attempting to raise the level of the conversation, or rather of her monologue. But I could tell she was getting more and more embarrassed at reporting things she thought I must find very shocking.) 'The wolves aren't so weak and hypocritical. Apart from that, what's the difference?' That's what he thinks."

He applauded any dictator who happened to be featured on television: Hitler, Stalin, Castro, Idi Amin Dada, Bokassa, Saddam Hussein. At first Alba put this down to irony, black humor: the half-heartedness of the previous regime was bound to have repelled a man as passionate as Vespasian. But his strategy was to oppose everything that wasn't himself. However, a continual stream of total trashing is no longer a real challenge; it becomes meaningless, idiotic, a torture to listen to. Under the influence of drink, Vespasian lost all restraint: vindictiveness made his eyes blaze, his voice grow hoarse.

"How hideous everyone is!" That was his constant refrain, even as they walked along the beach under the cypresses. "Especially the women! No charm whatsoever. Vulgar. And that includes your friend Stephie Delacour, whom you treat as if she was a film star. Round-shouldered. Clumsy. Don't you agree?"

This took me aback somewhat. Moreover I thought it in pretty poor taste for Alba to repeat such remarks to me. But I managed to muster up a condescending look.

"At any rate, they look better than I do," Alba would coyly reply.

"So what?" Vespasian naturally disregarded her appeal for a polite denial. "In the hospital, ugliness is normal. People are ill because they're ugly, and vice versa. But at least hospital patients have admitted defeat and gone to bed. Whereas people who are well . . . Just lumps of meat!"

As soon as Alba really understood this outburst it struck her as perfectly just. After all, wasn't everyone, in secret, really a monster? *She* didn't dare look for the craziness in others because she didn't want to find it in herself. But Vespasian was brutal enough to point it out, like a bright, uninhibited child. Besides, the Old Man said the same thing, though he expressed it in graceful images: his ghosts were unbearably polite. The simplest explanation, Alba decided, was that Vespasian felt personally threatened by ugliness, stupidity, and decay. So her only comment was a smile, though it didn't take long for this to exasperate him too. He hated mere silent approval: it was the typical pussy-footing of the weak!

"The phone!"

Good gracious, it's for Alba! Vespasian is annoyed, humiliated, he tosses his head like a dog that's been foiled of its prey. Is he jealous? Not exactly. But fancy anyone imagining there could be anyone but him on this number!

Anguish dilates the heart, then blood surges up to the brain and prevents you from thinking properly. Anger and the desire to cry out are replaced by weariness. So Alba's shouts were inaudible. Fatigue made her stoop and turned down the corners of her mouth. People wonder why some women age so early. It's because of unshared anguish. If Alba had had a child she would always have been either clouting or cuddling it. But she didn't have a child.

Still, Vespasian might have actually left her, mightn't he? Oh no! Public opinion may be stupid, but it's fussy as well. People might have thought it squalid if he decamped. Besides, the "Emperor" had to have a partner who was reasonably presentable. He'd rescued her, she owed him everything, so he vented his wrath on her and she meekly endured it. It was a comfortable arrangement; even erotic, sometimes. Those times had become rarer, though. Vespasian now kept his arousal to himself: he masturbated, or visited emancipated women who liked pleasure and didn't ask anything in return. People like Alba thought such ways of going on didn't exist. But they do! Vespasian at least was sure of it.

From then on, Alba merged herself with the passage of time. She thought only of what was to be done next—the next second, the next minute, the next hour, day, night, week, month, or year . . . She was caught up in an unremitting rush that left no room for sorrow or despair. Though wrapped up in the passing moment, she was indifferent to space because it existed in time. But there was no purpose in all this: she had no plans either for herself or for anyone else. Her one concern was to pack the present tight enough to absorb anguish; she somehow knew that the gathering pace of the ephemeral was bringing her closer to deliverance. To death? Why not? Meanwhile, she didn't think about it. She thought about only one thing: "afterward." Now it was no longer just a thought. It was her sole occupation.

5

Did she tell me all this or did I guess? I'm trying to sort it all out now, after leaving Santa Varvara—where I must admit my trip was a flop. But at the time, sunk in the yellow plush armchair with that interminable coffee before me and the fountain depicting Gulliver's wife down below, I became steeped in their story as in a pungent but familiar smell. Although I resented her diverting my attention from my own more serious concerns—my report on the political situation in a country that was continually flouting human rights—I felt myself being lured into the irresistible pleasure one derives from contemplating other people's troubles, however tedious. And there was more to come.

I could see how Alba's seriousness might be enough to bore any man to tears, let alone a man like Vespasian, though I personally found my gentle auburn-haired student of Suetonius very likable. But her husband now preferred the perpetual high spirits of a colleague of his at the hospital. She worked in another section, and he referred to her as his "Face-lifting Colleague," partly out of discretion and partly to minimize his real dependence on her. She was a strong character. As a matter of fact, as always happened when he tried to throw dust in people's eyes, Vespasian was only reformulating the truth. According to Alba, the Colleague performed plastic surgery on "patients" oversupplied with money but dissatisfied with their image. This class of customer was becoming more and more numerous, and would soon include all Santa Varvara's smart set. They spent their convalescence at seaside resorts, which, according to Alba "were quite deserted until just a few years ago—only foreign tourists went there, as you'll no doubt remember . . . I've had the pleasure of meeting our Professor in one of them—you've seen him again lately, I hope?"

I was finding it increasingly hard to follow the logic and even the chronology of Alba's monologue.

We were back again now with the Face-lifting Colleague, a character who symbolized the current atmosphere perfectly. She'd assimilated the general longing to start afresh so completely that everything about the hospital and the somewhat sinister goings-on there was an occasion for shrill laughter and maddening optimism. Even her face-job patients found it exasperating, though all they were after was a bit of uplift, if I may be forgiven the pun. But then they were in a position to see the gulf that sometimes lay between the Colleague's chuckling promises and the results of her ministrations. But Vespasian was never irritated, so determined was he to see nothing and approve of everything in the best of all possible vulpine worlds.

The Lady Face-lifter's euphoria allowed him to see life itself as the ever-increasing pleasure that an infant is entitled to expect from its mother. When he left her in the early hours of the morning to confront either Alba or some real patients, he regarded the resulting anticlimax as the result of a plot hatched by nonentities against their betters, those of a purer race. "The race of wolves," Alba would whisper, thinking of Septicius's ghosts. "So what?" Vespasian would brag, drunker than ever behind his mask.

While I was racking my brain about how to get an interview with the Minister of the Interior—my article was supposed to reveal the truth about some "unfortunate incidents" involving the Santa Varvara police—Alba had changed the subject. Not, however, before she'd asked me if I'd like to take a shower after I'd finished my coffee. "It's very refreshing after an exhausting night," she said rather sheepishly. I didn't disagree.

She went on with her story as she looked for some clean towels. I'd never noticed before how swiftly and skillfully the shy type of woman can let the family cat out of the bag: she'll tell you the most intimate details at the drop of a hat providing you're another woman and not paying her your undivided attention. In other words, provided you yourself might experience the same misfortune but are unlikely to interrupt her confessions with your own.

Alba had recently woken up to the fact that Vespasian had never really held or entered or tasted her.

"You think everything's all right, that that's just how it is. And then one day it hits you in the eye—or rather in the guts. That isn't it at all! Not that. Not at all. Do you see what I mean?" I wasn't about to tell her the surprises I myself had encountered in the pseudo-paradise of sex. But I believed I understood. Vespasian caressed, kissed, and penetrated her as if her whole body was wrapped in a huge condom. This might occasionally give them a somewhat wry pleasure, but never the total incarnation of one in the other—Alba's own expression—that transforms copulation into love. "All we've been doing is both irreproachable and insignificant": that was what Vespasian seemed to be saying—satisfied or sarcastic?—as he left her in order to go through the same motions with other women. "You're just polygamous by nature," his pals at the hospital chuckled. Vespasian couldn't make them out: did these dissolute fools imagine he had several wives? Hadn't they realized he didn't even have one? Alba?—she was only a smoke screen. He was forced to act like everyone else: it was only if you seemed to be an average kind of womanizer, like them, that they didn't try to pry into your secrets. Besides, he had no objection to having the little orphan girl under his thumb. She was quite agreeable in herself, too—pretty, and not stupid, people said. It was only to be hoped she'd stick to the role Vespasian had meted out to her.

6

By switching between hot and cold water I managed to stifle my yawns, and tried, with some difficulty, to follow Alba's frankly rather vulgar tale. It was beginning to make my head ache. Or my stomach—I can't remember which. She went on talking as she made me another coffee, and the incoherent narrative reaching me through the shower curtain was so naive I couldn't help feeling faintly disgusted.

"I'll have it just as hot as before, please, but stronger!" (I was washing my hair now, telling myself it was only natural to feel queasy after a sleepless night. And that the hot-and-cold treatment, plus a good cup of coffee, was the best way of getting rid of the psychological gunge a girlfriend may always dump on you if you don't watch out.)

"The whole town reeks of murder," Alba informed me calmly, looking me straight in the eye at last. We were sitting opposite one another in her little drawing room, after I'd dried my hair, downing several more cups of high-powered coffee as I did so.

"Is there any evidence to prove it?" (That was what I was here for.)

"A friend of mine. Septicius Clarus. Our old Latin prof." (Alba.)

"So?" (Me.)

"He says the people are turning into wolves. He says Chrysippus has disappeared. Chrysippus is never mentioned, and mass graves have been found . . . Septicius says the wolves are infiltrating everywhere." (Alba.)

"Has he seen them? Have you?" (Me.)

"Of course. Lots of people see them. Anyone who has eyes . . . " (Alba.)

"What about Vespasian? What does he say?" (Me.)

"He's changed . . . You won't recognize him . . . His face . . . The Old Man says he's getting to look like the wolves, too." (Alba.)

"As bad as that, is it?" (I didn't care for Vespasian, but even so . . .)

"Absolutely. He's become so . . . so forthright, shall I call it?

Especially when he's been drinking. He says he hates me and is going to kill me . . . And Vespasian may be very odd, but he never lies." (The cool way Alba was relating her marital woes ought to have surprised me, but I'd decided to disregard it.)

"Right, my dear, I have to be going now. But leave everything to me. And don't go worrying about that Vespasian of yours—this kind of thing can always be sorted out." (I was standing in the doorway of the apartment, saying the first thing that came into my head, about to go off and track down some contacts to wangle me an interview with the Minister of the Interior.)

"Yes. By death."

Alba's great eyes looked up at me one last time. I shuddered again at the loveliness shame had lent them, and fled down the stairs. After all, everyone had a right to a nervous breakdown.

I didn't know Alba was going to disappear.

When I emerged from the tower, Mrs. Gulliver's dislocated body still rose up out of the fountain. And I sensed more strongly than ever the impending violence that had been lurking out there from the start.

7

My inquiries weren't making much progress. I got to see the Minister of the Interior: he was courteous but inscrutable. Alba called me, but I didn't have time to see her that evening. Ten days went by like that: I hurtled around the new Santa Varvara's motorways in my rented Renault, armed with my tape recorder, investigating both individuals and whole apartment blocks—all equally standardized and uptight. But the interviews merely left me half dead with fatigue and boredom; they did nothing to remove my foolish but disturbing premonition of horror. What Alba and the Old Man said was true: people quarreled and shouted at one another in the subway and on the buses, their faces fierce and distorted; famished crowds waited in line outside the stores, exchanging insults. It was sordid and absurd, but I couldn't find a story in it. It was as if there had to be a certain amount of freedom around, as if things had to possess a modicum of grace, before they could supply material for even the most meager article.

As the cafés and bars of old Santa Varvara no longer existed, and the new city was so full of motorways you couldn't hear yourself speak, a number of new coffee shops and the like had been installed on top of municipal apartment blocks, away from the din. Onward and upward. They told me at my hotel the *Oasis* was the best of these places: it had air-conditioning. It was certainly an island of plush, leatherette and neon in the midst of a desert of reinforced concrete, asphalt roads, and gravel drenched in gasoline. But was it really an oasis? Perhaps, when you looked at the central area, where a slim fountain played in the middle of a dais rotating in a clockwise direction. Its seats were occupied by a lot of melancholy wretches tucking away enormous ice-creams and never addressing a word to one another. The nec plus ultra of kitsch. I needed a nice big scotch. "You don't have any scotch? . . . What about vodka?" "All right."

So there I was. The time had come to leave generalities behind. Every time I came here on a trip, Alba criticized me for taking too panoramic a view. She said I was wasting my talents. She was right. "Go for the microcosm, the detail, what lies beneath the surface," she told me. In short, my friend didn't think I was subtle enough, and disapproved of my rather blatant style of reporting, all show and no feeling. I agreed with her really. Alba's anecdotes might be more significant than all the weighty reports of Médecins sans Frontières or Amnesty International. I needed to go back to the grass roots. "What really matters, Stephanie, my dear," the Old Man had said to me just a little while ago, when we met by accident outside a supermarket, "what really matters is the microcosm—men's inner lives . . . and of course women's too."

Then he added with a sigh: "You won't have seen Alba again, I suppose. She's disappeared."

Upon which he vanished too, with what looked like panic in his eyes.

An unwholesome heat rose up through the dusty air outside the plate-glass windows of the artificially cool bar. The same unhealthy warmth as emanated from the faces of the people around me, hunched over their glasses. The heat of clammy, repressed thoughts without any means of expression. A sinister and oppressive atmosphere. A torrid silence.

I was just rummaging thoughtlessly in my purse for my lip rouge and my Opium spray when my eyes lighted on Vespasian, sitting in an ugly pink leatherette armchair on the other side of the room. He was wearing beige trousers and a loose tan-colored jacket, both made of one of those fashionable linen fabrics that crease whenever you move. His dark green tie brought out his olive complexion and acted as a foil to his jutting jaw and strong, prominent cheekbones. There was a dimple in his square chin. "The gigolo touch," according to Alba. He had a scar across his right cheek, mythical proof of his fight with the white wolf at the beginning of the invasion. His gaunt face, long thin nose, and thick crew-cut hair made him look excessively masculine. "Thuggish," I thought, and pretended to look at my watch so as not to meet his eye. (Five twenty-three. So what?) His eyes were bloodshot. I noticed how obsequious the waiters were when they brought him his drinks from the bar. Was it because he was a regular customer, or because he wielded a certain amount of power? Or both? What did it matter—he was the Emperor of the *Oasis*, anyway! He was also surrounded by a noisy court. Skulking behind my small pocket-mirror, I strained my ears to listen to his husky baritone. It sounded forced, as if he were talking to stop himself falling asleep. I gulped down the rest of my vodka —it reminded me of Alba: glowing, intense, and none too elegant— and made my escape.

Whiffs of jasmine and oleander mingled with the smell of sun-warmed dust, gasoline, and burning rubber. My editor had wired my hotel to say I absolutely must send in something sensational: some incident, some human-interest story to give readers an idea of the effect the invasion of the wolves was having on everyday life in Santa Varvara. He didn't want arguments: he wanted facts, simple facts. For once I agreed with him, though he was a complete idiot who was good at ordering other people around but had never written a single article himself. However, when I got back into my little Renault it had grown so hot I could scarcely breathe, so I decided to drop everything and go to the lake at Burgos for some air.

8

I'd caught sight of a crowd. That was odd. There weren't any stores in the neighborhood, so the people couldn't have been attracted by a special delivery of some rarity such as meat, coffee, or fancy tights. I went nearer. The grim, closed faces looked more distressed than usual. One old lady was sobbing. The men were conferring, with the combination of self-importance and callousness typical of incompetents. The body of a drowned woman had just been recovered from the lake.

There was a wound on her neck. "The wolves!" (The crowd.) "Probably stabbed by her lover." (One of the officious and insensitive nitwits.) "No—I saw fang marks." (The old lady who was weeping.)

The body was still lying there, covered with what looked like a tablecloth or a sheet. The police were on their way. No one must touch anything. I showed my press card and lifted up a corner of the cloth. Yes, there was a wound at the base of the neck. The long auburn hair was beginning to dry in the heat. Hair like Alba's, covered with water-weed and slime, and clinging to a blue and spattered face, unrecognizable because of the bloating and the mud. "Don't touch—we're waiting for the ambulance!" the old lady sobbed as with sudden energy she pushed me aside: she obviously regarded the body as her private property, only to be shared, if absolutely necessary, with the medical authorities.

It was the Agnes B. suit—black dots on a white ground— that was Alba's favorite. Imagine, at her age, wearing Agnes B. clothes, as if she were still a high-school girl or a 1968 student! Alba never did go in for luxury or the latest fashion; perhaps she couldn't afford it. She had just a minimal sense of style. I lowered the cloth.

"I know her!" (The young man standing beside me: shaven head, pimple in the middle of his forehead, not the sort to be overly impressed by a woman's corpse.) "At least, I saw her walking here by the lake the other evening with some guy."

The "clean" youth, with his unhealthy skin and dull eyes, didn't make a very plausible witness. But I pretended to play along.

"What was the guy like?" (Me.)

"Important-looking, you know? But an awkward customer too—he was shouting. Like he was angry." (The Clean Youth.)

"Yes, but what did he actually look like?" (Me.)

"Tall. Long nose . . . Oh yeah—and he had a dimple in his chin. It looked kinda funny on a guy in a temper . . . " (The Clean Youth.)

"Is that all?"

"I'm not a cop! Besides, it was getting dark . . . But wait a minute—yeah, he was wearing a green tie. Pale green, like a lettuce, see?"

"I see. Are you sure?"

"Are you from the police?"

"Almost . . . Hey, here come the big shots." That did it. The youth had seen the sergeant and his men arriving, and he wasn't going to waste any more time on me.

9

The Old Man's telephone didn't answer. Nor did Alba's. I couldn't resist the impulse to go round to her place.

On my last trip Vespasian had happened to be away, so I'd stayed with Alba for a few days. And somewhere in my voluminous purse I still had the key she'd lent me then. But would it fit the current lock? There's a greater element of chance in a journalist's life than you'd think from reading books: novelists don't dare say how great a part it plays. Anyhow, I was all right—the key turned, the front door opened. Inside, the apartment was quite tidy: the curtains were drawn; the standard lamps, with their subdued lighting, were still switched on; the table was set for dinner. How long ago had it all been left like that? I opened the eye-level, glass-fronted oven of the American-style kitchen, which formed an open plan (in my view, rather vulgarly) with the dining room. As I'd suspected: there was one of Alba's specialties—a dish of trout flavored with ginger—in the process of becoming uneatable. This was the only one of my friend's recipes that I'd adopted myself. It was one of the easiest: I marinated the trout in wine, port, or brandy; made a nice little sauce with oil, diced onion, and lemon; put the trout and the sauce in a dish with some finely chopped fresh ginger, then covered it with kitchen foil and put it in the oven. Twenty minutes and it was ready. Perfectly delicious. But Alba hadn't touched it. That was understandable enough. But apparently Vespasian hadn't, either. Hadn't he been home that evening? Or perhaps she'd gotten angry and gone out. On her own? Where to? No, he'd probably come home all right, but late. Insults had flown back and forth more violently than usual, they'd gone out together and continued arguing as they walked by the lake . . . And there . . . Possible, but unlikely. A couple having a fight don't make for the nearest lake to give their psychodrama a suitably theatrical setting. Why should they have gone out at all? Unless Vespasian had invented some story interesting enough to lure Alba down to the shore. At all events, one thing was clear: a dinner prepared in order to keep up appearances had not been eaten. And appearances hadn't been kept up.

I left the trout to its fate. Which was to rot in the oven. And to think it was one of my favorite dishes! Perhaps Alba, to cheer herself up, had cooked it for me to eat? Hadn't one of the messages left for me at the hotel been an invitation to dinner? When had that been? I hadn't got the note until the next day, when I got back from Burgos and the lake . . . And ever since then Alba's phone hadn't replied. Had just gone on ringing into the void . . . My tiredness had vanished now as if by magic. I sniffed. The smell of stale fish; and of ginger . . . Anything else? The mystery was deepening, and turning me into a detective. I *had* to see Vespasian at all costs.

I took a last look around the empty apartment. A book on chemistry had been left lying open at the chapter on "Poisons": the subheadings included arsenic, antimony, mercury, lead . . . A medical textbook probably, belonging to Vespasian. But was Alba interested in that kind of thing? She was more likely, in my view, to be studying books on tranquilizers and pep pills. Temesta, Lexomil, even Floxyfral and Cledial—people take what poison they can get. How could there be an ecstasy threshold that suited everyone? Some go in for fasting; others get high on suffering; Alba studied chemistry, another kind of cookery. In the end, frustration secretes the hormone of pleasure; apparently it has already been identified. Soon you'll be able to buy the appropriate pill in any pharmacy, even in Santa Varvara.

I put my key away carefully. I hoped I wouldn't need to use it again. At least, that's what I told myself. But I'd known for a long time that, whether I liked it or not, my fate was involved with the city of Santa Varvara.

There was a bottle of bourbon in my suitcase at the hotel. I spent the night with that bottle, and with the thought that I must find Vespasian. Must make him talk. Perhaps even sleep with him to make him do so. Make him drink. He'd be aroused but impotent, a feeble brute. There wouldn't even be any need for condoms—he'd tell me all just lying in bed without really making out. I knew a thing or two about these masculine types.

I didn't much care for this plan, but I couldn't see any alternative. Alba, if she was still alive, wouldn't ever know anything about it, of course, and nor would the Professor. And after all, taking risks was part of my job. No reason why I should be ashamed. I must just go to it and hit where it hurt. Even football involved risks: people imagined it was just a game, but it wasn't at all like ballet dancing. The same thing with an investigation. So why should I turn up my nose? That was my job. That was life . . . I finally dropped off to sleep. I didn't wake up till noon.

"It's between the two of us now!"

And I knew where I'd find Vespasian. At around five o'clock, at the *Oasis*.

5. No Point in Shouting for Help

1

"STEPHIE, MY dear, so it *was* you! I *thought* I saw you here the other day! . . . So—trying to find out what's going on in the great big world, as usual, are you?"

His eyes were bloodshot again. His once marked features were becoming curiously softened and blurred. Drink starts by dissolving people's faces before it makes them really old.

"Alba's gone away for a few days. Don't ask me where to— I haven't the slightest idea. She's very secretive, you know. Gone to see some friends of her parents', I presume. That lot always stick together. Of course you'll have dinner with me. Yes, yes—I insist!"

It all went as planned. The fish was completely tasteless and I kept on adding salt, lemon juice, and Tabasco—anything I could lay my hands on. At the same time I downed glass after glass of a wine that tasted as sharp and strong as brandy. Vespasian kept dabbing at his dimpled chin with his table napkin, a mechanical gesture that struck me as somehow salacious. He smoked a lot, letting the ashes drop on to his green tie and the lapels of his crushable tan linen jacket. I don't know how on earth I managed to seem seductive, but be that as it may we ended up in my hotel room for "one for the road."

I was sure, before, that a drunk scattering cigarette ashes all over the sheets could never give me an orgasm. But afterward I wasn't sure of anything anymore. And with Alba's husband at that! But of course, my poor child! Haven't you ever heard of the unconscious? Disgust has all the power of repressed pleasure. Under the joint influence of summer heat and our tipsy mouths, Vespasian's muscles grew strong again. He wasn't a skillful lover, but the amazing litheness of his body and the agility of his penis produced spasms in me that I didn't know I was capable of. And the more ashamed I was, the more pleasure I felt. In the midst of a nevertheless delightful frenzy I found myself hating us both.

It was the hot ash he dropped on my chest that brought me back to the object of the exercise.

"There are some funny things going on in Santa Varvara." (Me.)

"You mean the wolves? Mmm, apparently. But these things happen. Remember the rats in Oran!" (Vespasian.)

"I was walking by the lake when they fished out the body of a woman. She had a bite on her throat."

Vespasian was silent.

"Her hair was like Alba's, and she was wearing a dress like hers."

"Huh?"

He sounded worried. I'd gotten to him.

"She could have been Alba's twin sister." (Me.)

"How odd!" (Vespasian sounded even more disturbed.)

"It is, isn't it?"

"Have you ever felt like killing someone?"

"I don't think so. I don't know." (I hadn't expected this. I was at a loss.)

"I have. Would you like me to tell you a story? Here's one, then . . . You may have noticed I'm rather tired these days—I have dizzy spells. More than once I've nearly driven my car into a tree. So I decided I must try to relax. I also wander around the lake when I've finished at the hospital. Alone or with someone else—it makes no difference. Usually it's with a colleague of mine, a young woman from the plastic surgery department. She's very dynamic. And the least thing makes her laugh. Very good for the morale. As for the rest . . . Because we *are* going to tell one another everything, aren't we, Stephie my dear?" I hated him. If his lousy cigarette had set fire to his pubic hair and sent him up in smoke I wouldn't have lifted a finger to save him.

"One day there was a married couple, not far away. The classic confrontation. Jealousy, insults, tears, blows: the usual thing. The girl was rather like Alba, I grant you that. Through some strange vestige of chivalry, I felt I had to go over and intervene. But my Face-lifting Colleague is very wise—have I mentioned that? 'Don't be silly, my dear,' she says to me. 'You don't want to deprive them of their finest hour, do you? What if he is going to kill her? So what? In their lucid intervals, melancholics can act very badly, as you know. And aggression is still the only effective antidote to depression.' She always talks in generalities. It's one of her charms . . . So, as always, I agreed with her. When people don't believe in anything any more, what's left? Don't you see? It's very simple. Either nervous breakdown or war. Personally I prefer wolves to sheep. What about you, Stephie my dear?" (Although Vespasian had let himself get rather carried away, he hadn't forgotten about me. Neither had I.)

"I don't know. I've got rather a soft spot for rabbits: they run away. Not very impressive, I admit." (I'd lobbed back a little fable of my own: I wasn't going to let him take me by surprise twice.)

"No, indeed." (This was meant to take the wind out of my sails.) "This girl, this other Alba, was obviously one of the weaker types. She seemed to have spent all her time worrying, moaning and groaning, feeling sorry for herself —like most women, as I don't need to tell *you*. Your own dear Alba's the same. Always in a state either of lamentation or of moral rigor. Her Irreproachable Majesty showers *me* with reproaches. They're usually unspoken, but I can see them right away in the way she averts her eyes or purses her lips; even her skin prickles as soon as I approach her. My Face-lifting Colleague is right: I'm capable of killing that Alba of yours. Do you think I've done it already? Oh no, not yet. But nothing will stop me. I'm ready. And if you ever hear that your sad and gracious pal is dead, don't waste your energy looking for the murderer. It'll be me. Of course. No one will suspect, though, because I'm such a useful and responsible person; and *you* won't say anything because you're fond of me. At least in bed, I believe . . . "

Then he laughed airily, to make me think he was joking. But his eyes looked really sinister, I can tell you. After that I didn't hear any more; I lost all sense of time. What actually happened? Did we make love again? It's all a blank. Then slowly I began to hear his voice again.

"The man the other evening was in a beastly temper: he

killed the false Alba and threw her in the lake. And I had no quarrel with that. I didn't say a word. I haven't said anything to you, either, have I, darling?"

Vespasian was a cynic, but one can be frank as well as cynical: I wondered if anyone else had ever been really frank with me. I couldn't think of anybody just then, between the damp sheets flecked with cigarette ash.

To get back to the facts: had the Clean Youth confused Vespasian, a mere passer-by, with the murderer? It wasn't impossible. Unless Vespasian had simply invented the story to keep me quiet . . . Or unless he really had attacked an unknown young woman in a sort of trance, because she and Alba were as like as two peas . . . As for the real Alba, he'd just admitted he was obsessed with the idea of doing away with her. He might even have killed her already. In any case, his confession put him in the same category as the melancholy types who according to the learned Face-lifter—if I'd understood correctly— could only be saved from depression by rage. But the question still remained: why had he confessed so freely to his desire to kill? Why wasn't he more civilized? More hypocritical?

2

It really wasn't the moment for metaphysics. But lying there amid the sweat and the cigarette smoke I suddenly remembered something the Professor had said. For want of other ideas I'd interviewed him after seeing the relevant ministers and intellectuals. He may have been affected by the presence of my tape recorder, because he adopted the tone he'd used in the old days for those inspiring lectures of his. I was rather scared by this access of energy: it had a valedictory sound to it.

"Let's play a little game, shall we?" he suggested. "We'll try to find a phrase that sums up modern times—the era that came after Ovid, I mean. Two thousand years is a very long time, you say? On the contrary, it's nothing. I know my experiment strikes you as ridiculous, but just let's play for a moment—what other way is there of being serious? You don't feel you can risk it? Very well, *I* will and I venture to think you'll join me, Mademoiselle Delacour. Well, it's taken us twenty centuries to find out that in the beginning was hate. "Love thy neighbor," and so on. See Leviticus, Deuteronomy, St.Paul, St. John's Gospel, and the rest. But they've all been put in their place! The question is, can we still call the result civilization? Yes, certainly, if by civilization you mean that the hypocrisy of charity has been X-rayed and turned inside out; that in the devotion of the Good Samaritan we've detected the delights of self-loathing and hatred of others. Your friend Vespasian would say this should be a great help to psychotherapy. And it has indeed meant a great step forward for lucidity, though this doesn't suit anyone. People hate lucidity even more than they hate themselves: they'd rather cling to their illusions. But hatred hasn't merely been discovered, Stephanie; it has also become established. It's unshakeable, arrogant, unrestrained. It sees itself as truth, acting and speaking openly. I'm thinking of the wolves that are invading us, or that inhabit us, in the name of a cause—country, race, family, self, oppressor, oppressed, class, underclass, group, subgroup . . . "

"You look very pensive. What are you thinking about, my sweet?" (Vespasian was now using the familiar form of address. It's incredible the way some men think they can do this just because they've been to bed with you. He tried to kiss me.)

My only response was to pour him another whisky. But I could still hear the Old Man's voice.

"They're all hard nuclei, indivisible atoms that can only renew their strength by exploding against one another. Each has become a potential Hiroshima—but one getting closer and closer to realization. You say the modern world is a kind of spectacle. I see it as total war, a war in which everyone's fighting everyone else. A war motivated by the ego, without frontiers and without such paltry refinements as 'good' and 'evil.' "

The whisky slid down my throat like honey made from rye.

"We've lost the sense of belonging, Stephanie—forgotten the meaning of a bond. That's a tautology really—meaning is always a kind of connection. Don't think I'm asking for a revival of religion: these days religion is either worn out or vicious. Of course, the belonging that inspired the elegies of Tibullus or the tales of Ovid was a sacred bond both passionate and pious—by which I mean respectful. But it was also free, questioning, skeptical, intellectual . . . It was the dawn of connection. And that's the form in which we need it now. Not when it has become arrogant and acts as a kind of noose. Nor when it's dead, and leaves us free to die too, of hatred. I've spent my whole life seeking that dawn of connection, Stephanie my dear, and I'm more and more convinced it's still a long way off. Because for a long while we've been living in a kind of lingering midnight, which wakes up wolves and bats and fools . . . "

Old Septicius's diatribe, which at the time had struck me as too abstract for my article, took on a strange new resonance amid all the cigarette smoke and scotch that Vespasian and I were now ingesting. I felt the bittersweet pleasure of perverse satisfaction.

"We can't say or do everything," the Professor said. "But the people of Santa Varvara think anything is possible: motorways, dams, test-tube babies, forged invoices, stores that are empty, stores that are looted, murders, amnesties. They've turned into beasts; they've gone further than the wolves that invaded them; they're possessed by a desire for the impossible."

Vespasian longed for the impossible. That was what made him so horribly mysterious and despicable at one and the same time. He was inside me again, and I let out a moan, thinking I'd understood everything, whereas really I was a slave. But only for the moment.

3

I hadn't really understood much. For me, the strange relationship between Alba and Vespasian only deepened the mystery of Santa Varvara itself. I couldn't go back to Paris without solving the question of where Alba was. Mightn't the girl whose bloated body was taken from the lake be Alba after all? Vespasian had friends in high places: he might well have sabotaged the investigations. Corruption in this country being what it was, a cop might easily swear the victim was Y instead of X, and prove it too. I *had* to find Alba myself, dead or alive. Unless it was too late. The evidence about the drowning might already have been destroyed. Anyhow, I simply couldn't leave Santa Varvara yet, despite the heat and the fact that my stock of whisky had run out.

At this point the floor waiter brought me a thick envelope. Alba's writing. Incredible! I bolted the door, lowered the blinds, and drank a glass of water.

"Stephie, I've bored you to death with my woes, but I still haven't told you the most important thing. Why did I choose you to bear this burden, you who've been away so long you're almost a stranger? I don't know. I couldn't confide in the Professor—though it seems to me he's guessed everything anyway. He comes to tea with us sometimes, you know, in the apartment up above Gulliver's wife's fountain—partly by way of a change for himself, but mostly to provide us with a distraction. He soon saw the pass we'd gotten to. Vespasian's rudeness, his strange attacks of dizziness, my surreptitious reactions . . . I'll tell you all about it in due course. But again, why you? Because I love you, I think. At least, I don't hate you. So, in short, you shall know the truth.

"I don't think I need go into any more detail about the hatred that's now the only link between Vespasian and me. The silences that may last for weeks or even months. No sex, of course, except perhaps after a scene, with insults, slamming of doors, blows. He doesn't listen to me, doesn't understand what I say, doesn't come home except to eat, look at television, and shut himself up in the bathroom. He treats me with sarcasm and contempt in front of such friends as we have left. And so on.

"I ought to get a divorce, you say? What for? The men in Santa Varvara are all the same now. 'Wolves,' Scholasticus calls them, and I haven't the heart to try to find out if there's any exception to the rule.

"There's only one solution left for me, and that's slow death. Don't worry—I don't mean my own. I'm not suicidal. At least, not yet. I'm referring to Vespasian—to Vespasian's death. Every day I've been putting sleeping tablets and tranquilizers in his coffee, in his soup, in the salad dressing, everything. Now I've started to study real poison.

"A base kind of revenge? What's the difference between that and the moral and physical murder Vespasian has been inflicting on me? None. What I'm doing is even worse? Too bad. I don't say I don't feel any remorse. In fact, that's why I went away so soon after you arrived. So as not to have to tell you all this face to face. But I shall persevere, and no one's going to stop me.

"I used to love Vespasian: everyone likes to have someone else to lean on; no one can bear to live all on his own. But he crept into my silence like a wild beast. He's like a maniac—no one can stop him when he's angry. I'd like *you* just to see him for a moment yourself—and then go. I do all I can to avoid him: there's some terrible being inside him now that changes everything into fury, greed, and thirst for recognition. Is it possible for him to live with other people at all? I don't understand him. Isn't he like the rest of us? Doesn't he ever have any of those dreary days when you feel old and insignificant? Doesn't he ever suffer?

"When he isn't actually shouting out his contempt and resentment, his voice becomes quite flat and toneless so as not to betray his malevolence. The sort of voice you use to talk to birds in, because you're intimidated by the virtuosity of their singing. He never asks any questions, at least not of me. Mine is a life without questions. The opposite of an interrogation. A purgatory. An endless wait to hear oneself being sentenced. Perhaps to death.

"So I came to realize he wasn't really anyone. He was no one, not really a person at all. We think those who hurt us are devils. But no—all we see is a mask with no one behind it. It was when I knew this that I felt like killing him, not to consign him to his essential nothingness but so that he should have something happen to him at last. An adventure, a problem. I expect you think that's still just another way of loving him. Just wait a bit.

"At first I suffered a lot. Then I feigned indifference. And after that I really did become immune from pain. Insensible.

Made of wood or stone. And the poisoning is an invention of the woman of wood or stone I am now, for whom lethal drugs drop into food as easily, as innocently, as implacably as the leaves fall from a tree.

"Of course I neglect the house. Women who are loved arrange the furniture invitingly, and so on, like the seductresses they are. I have no one to seduce. My tables and chairs, lamps and curtains look as though they're in a depository. I don't water the garden any more, or prune the roses. I just pore over information about sleeping pills and narcotics—real poisons. I don't measure them out; I just pour a bit in and wait. Not that I'm actually waiting for anything more. I don't talk to anyone, even myself. Though I do let the Professor talk to me. Is it grief that makes me turn away from everyone? No, it's undying hatred.

"Vespasian still insists on my going to the hospital on special occasions. The senior consultants' birthdays. There's still a cast-iron hierarchy among doctors. Plus, in this case, the stupid convention of army rank. Not to mention the equally hierarchical vanity of army doctors' wives. It's as affected and as perfectly organized as a pantomime. Everyone acts his or her part, full of enthusiasm yet with great solemnity, careful to take precedence over someone else wherever possible, radiating false self-confidence. I do my best to find my own proper place, but I never succeed—I'm always doing things at the wrong moment, I feel more and more alienated from those hostile strangers. I thought I'd gotten over it long ago, but I still feel ashamed at being an outsider, not one of them. An upstart. Non-existent. Is it a question of pride? It was once. But there's no more pride left in Santa Varvara, because there's no more mobility. And if nothing's going to change, belonging or not belonging can no longer affect the course of events. At most it's just a by-product of the spectacle. The Old Man is one of the few people who still go on rebelling. His visions, his sufferings are a kind of denunciation. I listen to him. But I don't say anything myself.

"I'm no bacchante, and Vespasian isn't a bard. Killing him leaves me cold: hard as nails, tough, impassive. Do you remember the Edonian women who were changed into gnarled roots—another of the Professor's hobbyhorses?

"My own feet cling to the earth like roots. I try in vain to run away, but I'm stuck, I can't move. And when I try to find out where my fingers are, or my foot, or my fingernails—no point in shouting for help: I can see the wood growing up around my ankles. And if I try to make myself feel pain by hitting my own thigh, what my hand encounters is wood. My breast is turning to wood, my shoulders are wooden already. If I stretched out my arms people might take them for branches. And they wouldn't be wrong. *'Pectus quoque robora fiunt,/ Robora sunt umeri; porrectaque bracchia veros/ Esse putes ramos et non fallare putando.'*

" 'It has been a long time since the glory of the gods appeared to us.' Who said that? Since then only violence can delight us. Don't you agree? Look at the films everyone ingurgitates in the evening, slouching yet exulting in front of the television screen: planes being blown up in midair, mutilated corpses, legs blown off, and, in the background, neglected children and women drinking themselves to death out of frustration. But our jumbo jet is all the more wonderful because it will soon plunge into the depths of the ocean, the pilot strangled by perfectly acceptable gangsters, the whole incident full of the mystic cries of the victims. The wolves in Santa Varvara, as no doubt you've noticed, provide us with a similar kind of thrill. A whodunit that ends in a massacre. That's the kind of show that interests people. Otherwise they all go to bed.

"You didn't think I was part of all that, did you? But of course I am, my dear Stephie—of course! In my own way. Hating in silence, paralyzed with humiliation and yet at the same time ecstatic. For hatred is painless when you think it's justified. But can you think about hatred? As soon as you try to measure it you take away its passion and turn it into something invulnerable and unchanging.

"When I look inside myself, I find nothing but hatred. Did I catch it from Vespasian, or had I gotten it already? Like perfect love, invulnerable hatred is uneventful—it contains no surprises. But it's on the side of evil: it's totally oblivious of good and love, and they are totally oblivious of it.

"As I said before, if you think I'm frightful it's just too bad: the immobility of hatred is the hidden face of ecstasy. Remember what the Professor used to say: 'Not everything can be said—just try to remain unscathed!' He was trying to teach us to abstain from violent utterance and convert it into a kind of sober purity, invulnerable to all harm, equal to any test. Unfortunately he was so pure himself that he forgot about the power of passion. Which is always, basically, a passion for death.

"But revenge—whether wild and devious or dry and calculating—brings me no pleasure, I assure you. The only thing that can take the place of humiliation for me now is dull placidity. As I said before, I used to have some regrets. But now I'm just an absent spirit sitting in the dark. Turned to stone; dead to suffering; devoid of meaning; in the lowest depths.

"Weariness is probably the only symptom of consciousness I have left. You can't imagine how tiring it is, knowing all that's left of you is unfeeling hatred. I see myself as in the last stages of some moral cancer. I can't even say that this brute beast, this brute stone, is me.

"Keep this to yourself, dear Stephie. And try to think that, if I still try to share what I'm doing with someone else, perhaps I'm not such a criminal as I seem. Unless by sending this confession I'm trying to drag you into the dance of the wolves too?

"Alba."

4

Another glass of ice water and a couple more Valiums later . . .

Well, thought I, I wasn't expecting that, to put it mildly. Alba a murderess, and, as if that wasn't enough, sending me an emotional epistle stuffed with literary references, sham remorse, and ponderous introspection! That was all I needed! Who was killing whom in Santa Varvara, I should like to know? Vespasian's bloodshot eyes, his dizzy spells, his car accidents . . . Were they all due to the fact that Alba was poisoning him? I remembered her medicine cabinet full of mind-modifying drugs; the book open at the chapter on poisons beside the ginger-flavored trout . . . It wasn't hard to reconstruct the sequence of events.

Alba would have started by doling out generous amounts of sedatives and antidepressants with uncertain and unpredictable effects—the sort that naive psychiatrists and overobliging young assistants in pharmacies would hand over quite happily to the wife of a famous army doctor: Temestra, of course, but also Pertofran, Ludiomil, Tofranil, Surmontil, not to mention as much Moditen and Semap as she fancied; why not? True, these weren't actually poisons, but the victim soon shows signs of drowsiness, overstimulation, or depression, and that's enough, to start with, to soothe the alchemist's savage breast. But the subconscious is insatiable, and Alba would soon have sensed that these relatively innocuous potions wouldn't be enough. So then she'd have started to study real poisons: should it be arsenic or antimony, lead or mercury? Their physical and psychological effects, how long they took to act, how much suffering they caused—a Babel of unknowns conjured up by guilt and anguish before the fatal decision was made. But there still remained the most dangerous and thus the most thrilling problem of all: how to get hold of the chosen weapon. At first Alba didn't confront the question directly. Deliberately evasive, she didn't underestimate the charms of the researches involved, but she put them off, giving herself over instead to daydreaming about their results. It was enough, for the time being, to know that if you strike your prey in the mouth, the tongue, the throat, the stomach, and the intestines, he's as helpless as a baby at the mercy of unwholesome milk. But Alba didn't remember having been ill-treated by her mother. As a matter of fact she couldn't recall anything about her childhood, merely a dreadful void that suddenly began to throb with life, as if just being given form, with the beginning of her poisoned passion for Vespasian.

Clearly someone like her, in love with the twelve Caesars, wasn't going to be satisfied with a mere army surgeon from Santa Varvara. And though Vespasian's paradoxical nature tended to split up into several different tyrannical personalities, they were all lacking in substance and thus in grandeur also. Still, I'd never have dreamed that Alba's devotion to Imperial Rome and its perversions would fuel her hatred to such an extent, and turn her disillusion into so squalid a revenge. But that was what had happened. A modern woman, depressed, had succeeded where a paranoiac often fails: in killing her dethroned desire. But I was getting too pedantic. If I didn't watch out, my editor would complain—yet again—that he couldn't understand a word I'd written.

And the victim? . . . Why couldn't someone be both victim and murderer? Both the husband and the wife could play the two roles: wound and knife, cheek and slap, and so on. Old hat? But why not? Especially as it would make possible the perfect crime, the one and only, which no detective in the world could solve. If one took time to think about it, it was clear that if Alba died, and Vespasian killed himself, there would be as many reasons why each should have murdered the other as why each should have been the other's victim. I could feel my thoughts getting all mixed up. There's nothing like a murder, especially a murder among friends, for getting your logic in a twist, making you overlook the obvious, and producing the sort of brainteaser that would defeat the wiliest of sleuths. I must keep calm. After all, I did have overwhelming evidence against Alba—I was holding it in my hands. And I knew Vespasian's intentions. So I could actually prove simultaneously that both of them were guilty. On condition that I actually produced the evidence. Of course, they'd still need to die at the same time. This would call for the utmost skill, because, as with all couples, the point was for each to try to steal a march on the other. But why shouldn't Vespasian murder Alba, then die immediately afterward of the poison she'd administered to him? Pure hypothesis? Maybe. Of course, even so, if it weren't for my own two revelations—the one that had occurred during my night with Vespasian, and the one contained in Alba's letter—it could still be argued that they might both be victims of a third person. A wolf. But *could* I let on about my night with Vespasian? And *could* I betray Alba's trust? No, I certainly wasn't about to get into that game. Who would the wolf be then? Me?

5

I collected my red-hot Renault and drove as fast as I could to the old part of the town to see the Professor. If anyone could make head or tail of this carry-on it could only be he. I rang at the door. No answer. As I started to leave, I met the concierge.

"Are you looking for the Professor, mademoiselle? He's been taken to the military hospital. Yes—apparently it *is* serious. Yes, he'd been very worried . . . About a young couple, friends of his, who have problems, it seems . . . And then, of course, you know what's happening to this city of ours . . . Only the wolves will survive, and the Professor . . . You knew him quite well, didn't you? He wasn't really of this world . . . Listen to me, speaking of him in the past tense . . . ! But people like him, there aren't many of his sort left, are there? . . . "

The military hospital? Where Vespasian worked? And his Face-lifting Colleague? The Professor was in terrible danger. I was getting deeper and deeper into Santa Varvara crime.

It was not quite five o'clock on one of those clammy afternoons when the sun declined to pierce through the very mixture of confusion, dust, and smells that it was doing its best to cook up. Vespasian was probably at the *Oasis*. The Old Man's fate was now in his hands. Naturally, he wouldn't tell me anything. Any more than he'd enlightened me about Alba's disappearance. But I meant to see him and have a try.

Today the dais around the central fountain was rotating anticlockwise. It was still rimmed with churlish faces guzzling ices decorated with little flags and dolls and fir trees—the sort of thing that amuses children, and adults with nothing to do. Vespasian's usual seat was empty, though I could see the usual swarm of friends, hangers-on, admirers, enemies, profiteers, and gawkers around. And well, well—the Clean Youth was there too. He was trying so hard to look blasé and at home that he stuck out like a sore thumb. He seemed to be looking for someone, but pretended not to recognize me. I naturally acted as if I'd never set eyes on him before. Was it Vespasian he was looking for? Did they know one another? Did the Clean Youth know Vespasian? What if the killer of the girl in the lake was the Clean Youth himself, and he'd put himself forward as a witness so that he could hide behind a scapegoat? He looked quite capable of it, with his spotty face, his obsequiousness, his eagerness to find the murderer. Or perhaps he was Vespasian's accomplice—the perpetrator of a crime performed at the Emperor's instigation, an agent who hadn't received his promised reward, who'd begun to get his own back by almost denouncing his master, and who'd now decided to come and settle accounts once and for all. It wasn't impossible, but it remained to be proved. But where was this new hypothesis leading me? It would mean expanding the whole business, bringing in more and more people. Making things more and more difficult for myself.

One thing was certain: there was a growing number of victims in Santa Varvara, and I myself was confronted with three potential murders: of Alba, of Vespasian, and perhaps of the Old Man too. And I mustn't forget one person who definitely had been murdered already: Alba's double, the girl whose body was found in the lake . . .

The hospital was deserted. Visiting hours were over. "The head surgeon has left," they told me at reception.

Where could Vespasian be, since he wasn't at the *Oasis*? Had he disappeared too? I could understand it if he didn't want to see me. Or had Alba's spells already taken effect? Was an "inexplicable" car accident in the process of taking place, making the army surgeon look like yet another mysterious victim of the wolves?

I was told to come back again in the morning.

There followed a night of anguish such as I'd never known. A vast black space full of spasms. Hot sweats interspersed with fits of terror, putrid smells of dust and formalin. Words were dying, I was dying. There's nothing so impossible to describe as a nightmare in which you can feel yourself dying. All sensation is gone; you're the inert, helpless victim of a kind of abduction; and there's nobody left to register what's happening, only shreds of soon-to-be-putrid flesh. Something and nothing so close yet so disparate you can't remember them.

~ 6. Disparate Effects

1

THE THREAT of death was creeping into his skull like heat. The Old Man could feel it invading his visions, becoming at home in his visions as it was in his skin. That was something to be cheerful about.

He thought of the cheerfulness of people who didn't listen. Their mirth was fragile as soap bubbles. He himself was usually a good listener. He'd been lucky: you used to be able to see from his face that he was interested. But not any more. Now pain had replaced solicitude, taking up its position so smoothly he felt it had always been there.

Though charitable souls may think otherwise, the weak, the old, and the handicapped don't usually arouse pity. Both in those who rally round them and in those who keep well away, they provoke the distorted rages, the masked hatreds, the monstrous acts of vengeance that are revealed to us in our dreams, when the hypocrisy of day no longer operates. The Old Man had another burning sensation in his stomach. The vision disappeared, leaving only the sense of a wound that had gotten there somehow without his noticing. When suffering has destroyed curiosity, your sick "inside" doesn't belong to you any more—it becomes a kind of separate world with a life of its own. A life that looks forward to death.

He was alone inside a bubble of pain that didn't belong to him. It came from the wolves; it belonged to them. He himself felt cold, terribly cold. That was because he was conscious of being different, "other." But for how much longer? He didn't know if he ought to try to hang on to this cold. This wild and trembling difference—was it life itself?

The wolves, Alba, Vespasian, Santa Varvara, the concierge, the globe-trotting Stephie . . . He felt annoyance rather than pain at the thought of them all, and said to himself resignedly: "I wouldn't be missing much if I were dead." That being so, it was all right for him to give up the struggle.

But the screen of dreams doesn't go blank immediately when the body starts to withdraw toward the void. The organs may deteriorate; there may be tumors, hemorrhages; the chemical and electrical circuits may fail. But a kind of speech remains. Not necessarily articulate or audible or communicable, though it should be that too. And that pulse persisted stubbornly in the Old Man. It went on displaying a dream life that was fiercer and thus infinitely more living than his now enfeebled body. It wasn't that Septicius wanted to cling at all costs to a world that had driven him to despair, and from which the wolves had deliberately and finally excluded him. It was rather that he was now autonomous, detached from his departing body because of the artificial existence he had created for himself, from childhood onward, by learning to speak, read, write, and even identify with a dead language. Dead for his contemporaries, but for him a source of revelation, showing there was such a thing as the happy chance of being able to live in the mind.

What a strange autonomy it was, that interlacing of scraps of sight and sound unwatched-over now by any vigilance. Like some mad painter, the dying dreamer made pictures out of the hatred that was killing him, yet whose impact he was taming by absorbing into his own vision the horror of which he was the victim. In this way his cruel rendering of the scene became for him a new and temporary body, a prosthetic device made of signs that kept his decrepit carcass briefly but determinedly functioning. There on the frontier between the organs and the mind, between cells and images, the Old Man was amazed at the anger pervading the screen of his brain: it was time for that to end and for there to be peace at last. But after all, this black museum was his revenge. It was such a pleasure to see truth triumph, and he couldn't rub it into them enough what wolves they'd been. Or rather he could, but now, just as he was really in a position to show them the spider at the bottom of the cup, there was no one there to see or hear him. Not that they could do any more to him. Kill him? That was already taken care of. What still remained was the strength of those dark gray visions, before the death agony should come to upset the last pot of charred paint and freeze the final brush stroke of the visible, leaving the screen of wordless cells bereft of color, texture, all.

A blank.

2

But the film wasn't over yet: let the wolves come on, let them be seen. Septicius would take his etching tool and incise indelible images of them, taking pride in his pains. It was Lycaon he was after, Ovid's epic rage, the revenge of the humiliated. No more elegies, farewell Tibullus, lament would turn into caricature.

Brightness, distortion of space. Here an aquatint, there a painting. Septicius still had a thirst for knowledge; he meant to absorb every possible technique. You can't really learn properly until you're old, when you're neither gullible nor overeager and have a single, stubborn desire to burn all the oil that's left in the lamp. "I'm still learning," the Old Man liked to say. Stupidities, smut, bull-fights, craziness, sorcery—all manias and delusions are proper subjects for engraving. I loose my secret sorrows like packs of hounds against things and people. I tear them to pieces and shed their corrupt blood. Human passions?—a bestiary, a bestial carnival. Engraving is at its somber best when it's grotesque. Let's laugh at folly at last; at senile vanity, at witches with their birds of night and their fierce dogs—a mob of slatternly matrons flying a banner adorned with an ass's skull.

An obstetrician delivering dreams? Yes—if the sleep of reason begets monsters, that was what the Professor would be. Whereas people in general, whenever their common unity becomes ossified, want to be all the same, conformist, insipid, and neutral. But mightn't these dislocated animal faces be the invention of some latter-day phrenologist, a lover of ugliness, or an adept of the occult sciences, of secret cabals, mysteries, conspiracies, desires to reform or deform? Why not! Fancy was the only thing left to stand up to the prejudices that domesticated the wolves and made them seem ordinary and acceptable. What was to be done? Produce a rhapsody whose apparently contrasting elements really all vibrate to the same burden?: *No!* But should the choice fall on social satire, lewdness, or witchcraft?

On all of them at once, my dear Ovid. I borrow old Goya's palette to translate into dream what you once wrote by the Black Sea. For the Spanish painter, though deaf, was not blind to the stupidities, corruptions, and revolutions of his contemporaries, nor to anything else in the whole range of their rather unimaginative cruelties. These included the charlatanism of the scientists and intellectuals: nothing has changed. Alba and Vespasian are just some of the little fishes in that big swamp. Then there's the venality of lawyers still—the greed, the worship of appearances, the bribes and the amnesties, with everyone eager to get into the papers, but with no thought in their heads and nothing to say: all that ignorance and baseness. But whose? I'm talking of business men, bankers, doctors, artists, poets, musicians, painters, the vanity and frivolity of the ruling classes, the slack morals, the stupidity, the loathing of outsiders, and the corruption, the corruption, and the corruption again, of judges, parliamentarians, doctors, soccer players, industrialists, politicians . . . and I'm bound to have left some out. *These are the men who devour us. And what big teeth they've got!* But was Goya depressed? I myself am dying, embittered, melancholy, psychotic, beyond redemption. Perhaps one *has* to be at the point of no return in order to be a radical? I'm supposed to be afraid of sex, am I, to fight shy of grace, to leave women out of account? Poor old guy, they say—he's absolutely incapable of understanding swinging Santa Varvara and the contemporary scene!

Women! Dreary hypocrites, exploiters of men, lustful witches, surrounded by the modern equivalent of priests: doctors, psychologists, manicurists, psychiatrists, psychoanalysts, speech therapists, orthopedists, anesthetists. The profiteers battening on ignorance have multiplied and specialized: they have assumed masks, the better to exploit hysteria and its coven of cats and dogs, magic knucklebones and sinister dwarfs.

I'm exaggerating, you say? Perhaps. Women don't get on my nerves as much as they did on Goya's. Remember him on the woes of invasion, the disasters of war! You say you can't bear to look at such things, though you were born for horror, horror is your dream, and you try to turn it to your advantage, even though it's an unequal struggle. Does anyone still believe the human spirit isn't strong enough to transmit such a current of tragedy and contempt? Goya did it, and I'm having a shot at it too, even if I have got one foot in the grave. Look on it, if you like, as my last will and testament.

The dreams of dying men all paraphrase the same theme: consider the persecuted old age of Goya, the lewd old age of Picasso, the crazy old age of Septicius. Abductions, kidnappings, murders, swindles, violations of international law, invasions of sovereign territory, poison gas, germ warfare. Holy war! Terrorism offered up as a sacrifice to God! What next! You puppets, you bogeymen, you dumb beasts, you spiritual phantoms—you are birds of prey, but you're flying to your own destruction. You don't even belong to any particular age: a dictator straight out of the medieval Inquisition fascinates you, a liberal answers him in the tones of a Victorian puritan, while the common people cry out for peace. You're nothing but an empty space, a dud firework twisting and sputtering before it explodes: I set down your fizzles, I engrave your writhings. Whether you run away or attack, I'll be recording your half-

witted efforts. The vain vortex you live in is not merely plausible—Baudelaire was wrong; poets are incurable optimists—
no, it's real. Perfumed paradises are only a childhood memory.
A vision of the present is bound to be a vision of evil when it
proceeds from rejection—from a "No!" My rebellion is real: I
am dying of it. And still I say "No!" Until the screen goes
blank I shall go on etching on it the grotesque spectacle I see in
the world around me.

No!

3

The staff at the military hospital had taken away his
shantung suit. As if it were a concentration camp. Now he was
shivering in the rough standard issue nightshirt. All he had left
were the visits from his concierge, once a week. He was waiting for Alba: she still hadn't come, but she was sure to do so
before the end. The hospital—in other words, Vespasian—had
allowed him to keep his fountain pen to write to his daughter,
the violinist. But she had never heard from him: letters abroad
rarely reached their destination, and anyhow she was away on
tour.

He considered it his duty to use his pen to go on recording
things, to fight against his own slack stomach and waning energy. Alba would have thought the best thing he could do with it
was plunge it in Vespasian's heart. He'd been familiar with
death for too long to be afraid of it. But one day, feeling it to be
near, he wanted to go home. A man can't die among wolves.
There were no probes or cardiograms at home, but there
weren't any wolves either. Alba would have agreed. But Vespasian was keeping a close watch on the Old Man. For a few seconds Septicius felt afraid ; but he couldn't bear to be afraid for

longer. He was overcome with lethargy, which is a fear that counteracts fear, an attack that takes the form of inertia.

Outside the window the amber-colored poplars were like secretions of the moon: lunar rays solidified. During the night the heat abated, and the smell of flowers reached the Old Man through the dust. Was it summer, spring, or autumn? For someone who is ill, plant life has no season: it belongs to time itself; it is simply a symbol of endurance.

A sleepless night. Images crawling up to the surface of the brain and filling the retina with monsters.

The ads were the only thing he could bear to watch on television: they poured out heedlessly, affecting to know nothing of calculation and death. This, in a way, made them invaluable: they were life reduced to a bare minimum of hollow pretense. The glow from the screen widened his gaze and seemed to give him back his sight. The dying begin by losing the use of their eyes, and take to listening to their organs. But the Old Man was growing curious, although his curiosity had no object: it was just the tension of the pupils and the neurons as they reacted to the flashes on the TV. To all that pretense.

A face, either Vespasian's or the barman's, approached through the darkness as if backed by a blank screen left on by mistake at the end of the evening's programs. The Old Man perceived the face; he perceived his own perception, but without emotion; he perceived that his emotions were gone. The face—Vespasian's or the barman's—took advantage of this void to draw nearer, to grow larger. As it did so it lost its shape, became malleable: an expanding plasticine doll, a toy balloon swelling up to fill all space.

A flat nose, slit eyes, lips drawn back from ear to ear in a grin exposing black teeth. Two little bells held in the clenched hands made no sound. The knees were parted in what looked like a dance but might have been a spasm. Tucked like daggers into this Bogeyman's belt were two shrieking skulls: one hairy, with thick lips and eyes white with terror, the other almost bald, with jaws agape in a howl at some unseen torture.

The words flowed on until they gave way to a silence in which the image became blurred. It was the kind of almost waking dream that brings no rest but that reconciles the dreamer with its turmoil. When he awakes he is at once sullied and clean. Chaos was, but is no more. The past historic is the right tense for bad dreams that are over.

4

With what remained to him of consciousness, the Old Man wondered what century it was he was living in. " 'When the reputation of this dissolute age reached my ears,' cried Jupiter, 'I hoped it was untrue. But even the infamous report itself fell short of the truth.' " Who has not heard of the monster Lycaon?

"He, terrified also, flees, and having taken refuge in the silence of the countryside utters long howls in a vain effort to recover the power of speech; all the fury in his body is concentrated in his mouth; his usual thirst for murder is turned against the brute beasts; even now he still enjoys shedding blood. His garments change into fur, his hands into paws; he becomes a wolf. But traces of his original form survive: the same gray hair, the same furious countenance, the same glowing eyes. He is still a living image of ferocity . . . " "*Canities eadem est, eadem violentia vultus,/ Idem oculi lucent, eadem feritatis imago est . . .* " "One house only fell; but it was not the only house that deserved destruction. Over all the land the cruel Erinyes reigns; people will see it, looking back, as a conspiracy of crime."

"*Qua terra patet, fera regnat Erinyes.* 'The cruel Fury rules over all the land.' " Yes, that was exactly what was happening: "*Fit lupus et veteris servat vestigia formae.* 'Even as a wolf he still bears traces of his former shape.' " There, outside. There, all around the Old Man. Lycaon, Vespasian, Alba, the nurses, the Face-lifting Colleague, Gulliver's wife's fountain, wolves, werewolves, wild men, waste, muddle, mess. All was lead, lucre, lugubriousness. Where was the light?

Was it murder or make-believe? Crime or show business? What century was it? Was he in the first century, in exile on the shores of the Black Sea, dreaming of the metamorphoses that took place in human beings as they entered upon a new era, a new age just as steeped in brutishness as the old? Or was he in the present, in Santa Varvara, where a Bogeyman would soon come and disconnect the artificial lung that was still keeping the Ovid-haunted ancient alive?

The screen began to flicker, the green light fell on the Bogeyman and he disappeared. But the darkness went on deepening, and the Old Man could see, there by the rustic-style chair with its faded loose cover, an animal swathed in a white sheet. It was clutching the cloth to its chest like a modest person getting out of the bath and letting a towel remind him of the shape he has just been surrendering to the water. The beast's muzzle poked out hungrily, meanly, over the folds in the cloth, like that of a rat grown to wolflike proportions. The Old Man knew that expression: it reminded him of the sham politeness of someone at a lecture, disliking what he hears but pretending to follow, while in reality preparing to attack the lecturer with caustic questions at the end. The Old Man had witnessed this scene several times before, but tonight the rat-wolf was biding its time by the chair while a horde of bats, monkeys in wigs, and witches in chadors gathered around it.

The heat wave was over: a storm rumbled at last outside. The greenish-yellow rays of the forgotten television set began to sweep away the image that had been forming on the dying man's retina. It was then that the most sinister scene of all appeared, leaving the Old Man petrified on the edge of the bed. Two creatures that in another life might once have been a man and a woman were crouching naked on the carpet near the window overlooking the street, from which rose the smell of tar, dust, and jasmine. They both had asses' ears, but their sleek, furry cheekbones lengthened into muzzles, with lips drawn back to reveal the fangs of wolves. The woman was old and holding a bowl of boiling pitch, into which her companion was about to dip a paint-brush. What for? Well, these erstwhile humans had caught a real wolf, now a wretched prisoner, gaunt and desperate, and the wolf-man and the wolf-woman were tearing the animal apart, basting it, stopping up all its orifices with the hellish brew in the bowl.

"How obscene!" (The Old Man, waking up in horror.) "You've been torturing Goya!"

But the nurses had all gone away and there was no one to hear what he said. In any case, would anyone in Santa Varvara have understood it?

5

Two disparate shadows, the same as those a little while ago, were now prowling around the artificial lung. An emergency. The Old Man was having difficulty breathing. "Oh, leave me alone! What's the point of harassing a heart from which the blood is already ebbing away? Do me a favor and let me tread the path I have to tread in peace . . . "

The shadows took flight. The Old Man, though he couldn't speak, went on thinking.

"Even when I was only a child my heart shunned you, you great perverters. Its inner love made it incorruptible: its devotion was to the sun and the air . . . "

Night. He couldn't breathe again. He tried to call out, but no sound came from his mouth. He felt for the bell and rang it for some time. He wasn't afraid of death, but it was annoying to end like this, surrounded by the wolves. No one came. The nurses were playing cards, or drugging themselves with porn or books on the occult. No thought there. No chance of getting at *them*.

The dying may lose their memory, but sometimes they are filled with joy—childish or sexual or even foolish joy: the last remains of what was once energy and is now seen by onlookers as merely senile. Just as the fluorescent square of the television set was swallowing up the apparitions and merging with the moonlight, the voice of Billie Holliday overwhelmed the Old Man's ear and all his organs. It sounded now husky, now shrill; it was full of sighs and strong rhythms. Physical perfection.

He heard it with his body, with solemn jubilation, bone and muscle, greedy clarity. If all the other senses had had to be metamorphosed into sound, they'd have chosen to be embodied in the ghostly voice of Billie Holliday—there beneath the limes around the dance floor, by the lake where the wolves loved to lurk. The Old Man, who regarded music as the most ineffable and thus the most sacred of secrets, would never use his own voice for anything but hymns and suchlike. But he had cherished in his bosom one profane secret too, and Billie Holliday was its lewd priestess. "It's foolish but it's fun." Lascivi-

ous innocence. Perfection of sound joined to precision of pleasure—that was Billie. A groan of anguish rising up into a pure
and laughing vibrato—that was her too. And when the Old
Man relinquished his hold on life, and his one remaining memory of happiness sought to inhere in a form both rapturous and
insubstantial, it was the voice of Billie Holiday it chose. *"I
have a long way to go."* Death sometimes allows virtuous old
men to know again the pleasures of youth, suppressing all their
hurts and leaving them with their finest mental ecstasy. Some
myths speak of men being conceived through the ear. The Old
Man was dying that way.

6

I got to the hospital too late. Vespasian, officious but
almost inaudible, trotted out the report to me: they'd tried
everything—oxygen tent, artificial lung, cardiac pump, the lot.
He wore the sheepish expression of someone who's lying, and
never looked me straight in the eye. Alba had rushed over a few
hours before the end: did the Old Man know her? She wasn't
sure; she was ashamed. More ashamed than ever. Toward
whom? The Professor? Me?

It had been in everyone's interest to get rid of Septicius
Clarus. His death suited the people of Santa Varvara because
he spoke out about the evil everyone else had learned to live
with. It suited Vespasian because the Professor knew he meant
to kill Alba. It suited Alba because the Old Man had guessed
she wanted revenge. It suited the Face-lifting Colleague
because she couldn't stand people who were sad. It suited the
nurse because she was badly paid and had had enough of changing all these old fogies' diapers. It suited the wolves because
they were wolves.

But who had disconnected the artificial lung? Nobody? Was the embolism he'd suffered inevitable? Perhaps. I didn't believe in chance any more. There was no such thing as chance in Santa Varvara. Someone had committed a crime in which everyone else had collaborated. I was convinced someone hadn't been prepared to wait for my old Professor to die slowly. That someone had taken steps. But who was it? Vespasian, because he thought it permissible to eliminate the weak and because killing gave him pleasure, as he'd told me while taking his pleasure of me? Alba, out of humiliation and the stony ecstasy of her hatred? A wolf, disconnecting the vital tube with its paw? In any case, it wasn't me. Everyone was suspect except Stephie Delacour, and she wasn't even going to be able to tell the story in her paper. What was there to tell?

The night when a friend, a lover, or a father dies is somehow improper. You don't know of your loss, or who it is that's dead. You may be uneasy, but you're not unhappy.

I dreamed about Paris that night. There's some subterranean relationship between us. It was raining, nothing was happening, I was at a loose end. But I had an appointment with the city itself. The subway was my accomplice. It took me to Montmartre, Barbès, and Clignancourt. I changed trains, was sometimes underground, sometimes out in the open and on viaducts; I didn't need to know where I was going—when I'm in Paris I'm just going around it. Someone tried to take me hostage and send me back to Santa Varvara. I was frightened and clung on to my blue seat on the RER, the high-speed métro serving the suburbs. I felt safe there; if only I could just go on speeding through the darkness with all those poor tired people—*they* wouldn't let me be taken away. Unless the wolves managed to get here too and cut off the current, change the driver's face, carry me off to Santa Varvara and the lake, to Gulliver's wife's fountain and the military hospital . . .

But no. It just went on raining; we were approaching the university halls of residence, I was flying over the Parc Montsouris, the leaves of the trees were sparkling damply in the drizzle, I drank in the moisture and the pungent smell of the train; I loved it all. This journey was my dream of home, the base I carried about with me through all my travels. When the dream revisited me in Santa Varvara, I knew I'd had enough and I was going to go back. Dreams of space are worse than actual nightmares: they have you roving through anguish in hope of nothing.

7

The old church beside the house where the Professor had lived couldn't hold all the people who flocked to the funeral service. Among them were most of the local swells, very youthful-looking after their face-lifts but with skins so taut they couldn't have shown any grief if they'd tried. The barman from Burgos, who'd picked some branches from the lime trees bordering the dance floor, was clutching them against a threadbare black morning coat. The concierge was weeping into a bunch of cream-colored roses. The priests intermingled their lamentations with swirls of incense so pungent a little boy fainted away. I wondered if I wasn't going to do the same.

But now was the moment to keep my eyes open. The murderer was bound to be there in the crowd, and if *I* didn't find him he never would be found.

For a few hours the animals had reverted to human form and come to contemplate one of their number who hadn't played the game. This made them very circumspect. Almost noble.

It may be that death, with the fear it inspires, shows people they have a soul. Certainly mourning with all its paraphernalia may be more imposing than simple joy. But this crowd wasn't in mourning. It was just that, in the presence of the incorruptible, they all felt as if they were being judged. In Santa Varvara, where laws were made to be ignored and judgments, whether first or last, resembled hatred and folly, the church, full of flowers and musk and incantation, was secretly changing into a courtroom.

But there was no prosecutor and no prisoner. Only a victim, flowers, hymns, and the scent of cinnamon. No one believed in what was going on: to them it was just another spectacle. Yet everyone succumbed to its influence. For a few hours they were metamorphosed again, but in reverse.

When everything is forbidden, nothing is prohibited. And it's not much worse when nothing is forbidden. Wherever the unconscious rules, barbarism prevails. But if amid this hell just one person remains conscious of what lies behind appearances; if there's a single visionary who can perceive the extreme limits of being, where it may be corrupted and degenerate into brute force—then the others may recover their original shape.

So the wolves returned to human shape around the corpse that they themselves had "suicided." They had a suspicion that they might be reprehensible, might have done something wrong. They didn't feel guilty or sinful, for none of them was a believer.

Alba and Vespasian ostentatiously avoided me. They went about hand in hand, perhaps because they were reconciled, perhaps merely because they were accomplices.

There was no sign of the Clean Youth, of course: one doesn't mix up the social classes, even at a funeral, even in Santa Varvara. But a woman wearing a permanent smile did keep trailing my two friends ("criminals," I almost called them to myself, but as you can't have a crime without proof I dubbed them merely "suspects"). She was a handsome mature woman with so much poise, or arrogance, it was difficult to guess her age. With her silk dress, neat chignon, and expression of tolerance tinged with irony, she seemed to be suspending the harsh sentence we all deserved: she was a woman of experience, and was kindly going to forgive us. Was she a former schoolmarm promoted to head teacher? Or housekeeper to some noble family? A Professor at Santa Varvara College? The manager of Balmain's perfume department? Of course not. She was the Face-lifting Colleague.

So the threesome now showed themselves discreetly in public. It seems a couple needs to have a third person around if it's to last. When that third person isn't God (the most reliable cement for keeping families together, though apparently growing less and less able to withstand the assaults of sex), it's a Clean Youth (though such idylls soon become suspect) or a mother-in-law. The sacrificial matron, who rules over one of the two protagonists and adopts the role of stepmother toward the other, directs the war between them until death doth them part or they split up. In a more positive but very much rarer variation on the same theme, she is the apex of a triangle that keeps the other two in equilibrium; the good fairy with whose aid what was previously a couple becomes a mechanism for triple survival. So had the Face-lifting Colleague successfully performed one of her most difficult operations—a nip and tuck of the partnership between Alba and Vespasian? But how? I didn't know if her own perpetual smile was due to surgery or to the good humor that never left her, even in—*especially* in!—the presence of a corpse. I was so taken aback by the mask she wore I couldn't begin to guess what it concealed.

I must have kept some of my wits about me, though, for I noticed some curious scratches on her otherwise well-groomed left arm. They were like the scarifications that people living alone with a dog or a cat will sometimes let their pets inflict on them, and then try to conceal. Perhaps she lived with a wolf. No perhaps about it. The Face-lifter was a pro: this imperturbable maniac, so beautifully turned-out, so unmoved amid the mourning that engulfed the rest of us, was quite capable of living with a whole pack of wolves. At all events, she was capable of controlling, domesticating, training, and making use of them. And of emerging unscathed—much more unscathed than my poor foolish Alba, who was just a novice, for all her boast of stony insensibility in that ridiculous letter. Witness her red eyes now: she'd been crying again. Not, I know, that weeping makes a criminal any less guilty.

I mustered up my courage and went over to her.

"So what about that trout of yours?" (Me.)

"Did you call in at the apartment?" (Alba.)

"I was worried." (Me.)

"For once." (Alba).

"Don't be so difficult." (Me).

"Vespasian didn't come home. He . . . he's rented a studio . . . For when he's tired . . . or has to work late . . . " (Alba)

"I see." (Me).

"So I went away for a bit." (Alba).

This was so much like an entreaty, I refrained from reacting.

"To the provinces." (Alba.)

"That poor trout. Left to stew in its own ginger . . . " (Me.)

"Poison! Eating's a luxury for the simple-minded." (Alba.)

"I must be very simple-minded then, my dear!" (Me.)

"I'm not, any more." (Alba.)

"So I saw. So I read." (Me.)

"I'm sorry. Forget about it." (Alba.)

"Of course." (Me.)

For the first time I found myself not believing a word Alba said. My mistrust sent cold shivers down my spine, but there was nothing I could do about it. It wasn't credible that Vespasian would have passed up a good dinner, nor that Alba would have left the results of her culinary sorcery to take place without an audience. And this cold, terse way of talking was not at all like her . . .

I couldn't get the Face-lifting Colleague's scratches off my mind. She must have hated the Old Man. Or rather, with a typical quack's ambiguity, she must have wanted to relieve him, to free him from his now pointless life. No medication for the old except vast doses of old-fashioned or past-sell-by-date drugs, or water, or placebos, or nothing at all, until you actually switch them off. But in this case someone noticed, fought, struggled. Was it the Old Man himself? Given the fury of his visions, that wasn't impossible. Or perhaps it was Alba, faithful to her Latin? Or Vespasian, overcome by remorse? No, Vespasian would have been on the same side as the Face-lifting Colleague from the beginning; it was an obsession—do or die! Anyhow, the Colleague had been clawed and bitten, but not stopped. Plastic surgery conquered illness, a pleasant image hid old age—so why shouldn't it hide death? Death doesn't exist any more, let's send in the wolves instead and pretend nothing has happened. She kept on smiling: no one noticed how monstrous it was. The laughter of a hyperefficient madwoman is always regarded as acceptable. I was sure the others would imitate it that very evening in front of their halogen-lit mirrors, pulling all sorts of faces to arrive at the right "look."

And after all, why should I assume they felt they'd done wrong? Maybe they were just relieved at not having been found out; at being able to go on performing their wretched tasks with impunity. And, from now on, without any witnesses. For the Professor was no more. And I, Stephie Delacour, was about to leave—I'd had enough, both of their wolves and their problems. But I'd be back. Later on.

For the time being I needed to think about the Old Man. I suddenly felt like writing up my memories of my own old man, my father—yes, really!—which were now coming back to me. They'd been revived by the suspicious death of the Professor, whom in fact I'd hardly known at all. Which should I write about?: the Old Man or Papa? This was my way of feeling guilty, or, even more pretentiously, of being sensitive. The elegies of Tibullus? I could write them too. It was very seldom you met someone really human. By someone human I meant someone with vision instead of the almighty reason that could justify anybody in getting rid of anybody else. The only thing was, you couldn't really call all this an event, a "story." My editor wasn't going to be pleased. I could hear him already: "So our roving reporter, our great detective, is stumped!" Let him laugh, then. I had a right to my own whims and fancies.

Part Three

CAPRICCIO

⌇ 7. By the Throat

1

THE FACE was translucent and radiant despite red marks due to the martyrdom of intensive care. The brightness and peace of the cheeks, the restfulness of the lips, the eyes sunk back in their orbits as if drawn by some inner song, all combined in a sculpted smile. Apart from my father's, the Old Man's was the only corpse I'd seen smile.

He was no longer of this world, and neither was I. I was under no obligation now. And no one could intimidate me. But my grief implied a kind of respect. For whom? No answer. I'd have liked to smash everything up, but such blasphemy suggested some lingering concern with morality, whereas I was more of a quietist if anything.

My lips on the icy skin. People think a corpse is frightening;

that there's something horrible about the chill of a dead body. But they're wrong. Beneath my kiss, this one was alive, cool only as if it had just emerged from a session of scuba diving. I might have been refreshing myself with an ice, an Eskimo, juxtaposing the glaciers of the Frozen North with scented church candles. We two were opposite poles: but drawn to one another, inseparable. There was neither life nor death; just him and me. An old woman extracted me from that long farewell; or rather prevented us from departing together. Old women may be stupid sometimes, but they know death and love are two sides of the same coin.

He was weightless, with a presence unparalleled except by the solid insubstantiality of words. He didn't take up any room, and yet he enfolded me, kept me on the right path, consoled me. So much so that when he died I collapsed and tried to bury myself in a ceaseless, stupid round of work that was punctuated by continual colds and sore throats. I thought I was over it when my editor drove me to the limit for the umpteenth time; but after that one outburst I relapsed into a state of dreamy hallucination, my own brand of madness. I forgot that Papa was dead. But he wasn't dead. He couldn't die, any more than words can. Just try! You can silence everyone, burn all the books, cut their pages to pieces with scissors, do anything you like, and you'll only find that if someone has heard something even once its meaning will survive. Its survival depends on the someone who heard it. And I had heard, and continued to live on, a dream of immortality, of death denied. The fact that someone couldn't be seen didn't mean they didn't exist. The less I saw him the more he existed, with a presence that was immediate, out of time. Mourning couldn't touch me. Believers are never really bereaved.

The Old Man had to suffer the brutality of the wolves, I had to witness the hatred between the living inhabitants of Santa Varvara, and Alba and Vespasian's physical metamorphosis, before I woke up to it at last. To the fact that his body had gone, that he wasn't there any more. Papa was really and truly dead, and no one could ever take his place. Death had forced me back to square one, and square one was empty. I was a detective in search of the void.

2

His arms reached out into space, his breath saluted the wind. And he wanted his daughters to be like him—to be of the air. Nothing simpler: we must be athletic. We'd start with arm-circling, back-stretching, knee-bending, flexing the muscles of stomach and thighs. What a bore; I was exhausted as soon as I'd begun. Just another ten minutes, and our bones would be allowed to relax in a "Greeting to the Sun," a reward Papa saved up till last. If God had been a sun I'd have believed in Him, because of my Old Man. I'd stand with my hands together, head raised toward the still red globe of morning, bend forward and place my palms on either side of my feet, stretch my legs out behind me, stick up my rear end. "Keep your back flat, hold your breath, head on knees, stomach in . . . Now breathe out as you straighten up, and thank the sun for having passed through your body." But who was it really who'd passed through my body? The sun, or myself? And who was I? I didn't know who you were, Papa—a ray of the sun? a sigh? I'd have liked that pseudoprayer to a pseudosun to last for ever. Meanwhile Victoria would giggle and give up. All right— that'll do, then! And we'd both take off as fast as we could. What did we care?

You'd stay on, downcast, by the sea that they call black but

that is more vividly blue than any other. But it's tough and tur-
bulent too, with waves like granite. You often looked like
that—a bit upset—but it was only a fleeting pain: your gray
eyes contradicted it. Not that they actually laughed. They just
looked into the distance with an intensity, almost a cheerfulness, which might have been taken for hope. What were you
hoping for? A ray of sunshine? A sign from me, Stephanie Delacour? I was running off toward the waves, not to pray, but just
to lure the reluctant Vickie as far as I could out into the water
and make her race me back to the shore.

3

He folded up the small garments Mother had washed
and ironed and set aside for the trip. Father was the only one
who could pack a trunk properly, with everything lying flat
and elegant, to emerge without a crease at the other end. A fine
art, let me tell you. No one else tried to interfere; we just left
him to his monastic perfectionism. And all that just for one
sooty night on a train that made Mother feel sick. She'd sit
there pale and limp as the clothes in the trunk, holding a hand-
kerchief soaked in eau de Cologne to her nose and mouth.
Then there we were, by the sea at last. We could see it from the
station. Then off we'd go again. The harbor, the boat. Another
five hours, hours of pitching and tossing on the wild waves.
What an adventure!

Everyone was throwing up, was about to throw up, or had
just finished throwing up—until the next time. Everyone
except Victoria, who was gloating. She didn't feel a thing.
Mother had vanished into the cabin: no one was to bother
about her, she couldn't stand being fussed over. I'd thrown up
all I could, and was now holding my breath to keep my stom-

ach from heaving. Innards were supposed to stay inside you. But oh no! Their one idea was to pop out. You only had to cross some sea or other to find out: there was no holding them! Everything I had inside me would burst forth if I didn't hold my breath and hold down the black sea swirling about within.

Father was beside me, trying to help. Trying to say something reassuring, I supposed, in between his own gulps. What with all this and his ulcer too, he must have felt awful. But I never actually saw him throw up. He managed to feed the fishes and go to the toilet somewhere or other out of sight, and at the same time, hiccuping wanly, to keep mopping my mouth and forehead with a damp sponge. "It's nothing, really—even sailors are like this to start with! It's a baptism not of fire but of water—Neptune insisting on having his due!"

I hated Neptune, but clung to Father and kept my innards safely down.

Phew, what a relief—we were nearly there! The siren of the boat—it had behaved more like a seesaw—split our eardrums and soothed our last qualms. "It's a paradise—you'll see! And you'll have earned it!" We were in Santa Varvara. Paradise or no, why couldn't I just have been born there instead of having to earn it!

Father hadn't been born there either, but he took us off on this wild adventure with him. He believed life should be full of experiences, journeys, discoveries. I thought so too. I went for walks, I pawed at the ground, I ran about in my little sandals. Sometimes I slipped and fell. The scraped knees and stubbed noses I suffered! The gallons of seawater I swallowed in order to become a genuine explorer of the rocky, weedy waters of that seaside resort near Santa Varvara! And the searing sunburn! But let's say no more about all that. Our family must have been made for that paradise; even Mother finally came to believe in it. She smiled, anyway. If we were going to be ambassadors to Santa Varvara, we had no choice!

4

They were making the embarrassing noises children all think their own parents incapable of. Other people's parents, perhaps . . . "Gently—it hurts." "Just once more . . . you *are* sweet." "No—careful!" "All right." And so on. The heavy breathing of lovers, of coarse and noisy brutes. We were supposed to be asleep. They might have been more careful! Or have gone somewhere else, to a hotel, say, or at any rate not just on the other side of the wall, or not while I was there, anyway. Or they could have just kept quiet and gone to sleep like everybody else.

I wanted to shriek out, smash everything, say nothing, melt away with embarrassment, kill them. The last thing I wanted was just to doze off. But how could I get away? I couldn't move; they'd have heard me. All I could do was cry, just cry, soundlessly, devoured with unshed tears and passion and rage.

I don't know what night it was that I had my dream—"Stephie's dream" everyone called it, so famous did it become. I'm inclined to think, now, that I dreamed it before rather than after that squalid overheard scene; I may even have dreamed it several times. But after listening in on that scene more than once, I finally had the nerve to serve my dream up to *them*. Just like that: innocently, slyly, not really knowing what I was doing, but not without an inkling that my story might be a bit risqué.

A train was tearing along—a train as huge and fat as the engine-driver who drove us to Santa Varvara. And it ran over Father's throat and cut his head off. God knows how poor

Father got on to the rails—he didn't have suicidal tendencies. Had someone pushed him? Anyway, his head had come unstuck from his body—severed was the word. No blood. I kept that to myself.

The family thought it was stupid—thought I'd gotten it out of one of the strip cartoons I used to revel in in those days. But the next day Father did have a bad sore throat. A horrible one that lasted several months. At least, that's how I remember it. He used to cough and spit blood. "Only a bad attack of pharyngitis," he used to tell Mother, who always feared the worst.

My train remained stuck in his throat for a long while. He was always coughing afterward. I don't think he ever stopped. And the Old Man fell sick when the wolves invaded Santa Varvara. Now *I* wanted to feel ill too. What a laugh. What a slut.

"A man's not a father till he's dead," sages say now. They don't know what they're saying. In the past, people like my father—foreigners—or oriented toward a past culture, like the Old Man, set such a gulf between themselves and us that their goodness reached us as if from beyond the grave. Their serene otherworldliness crystallized my youthful, perhaps even feminine anger against authority and highlighted my anguish. So I either challenged or disobeyed them, or else tried to escape by trying to be even better than they wanted me to be.

The detachment of the fathers exasperated the wolves and whetted their hunger. They invaded the plains and the cities in droves, more ravenous than ever, deadly, contagious, spreading an epidemic that left people with human form but wild faces and bodies that gave off bestial stenches. You couldn't help wondering whether it was the serenity of our fathers, who'd always seemed to us as good as dead, which had acted as a magic spell to conjure up the wolves; or at least to bring hitherto civilized hysteria out into the open. In other words, whether the wolves would have emerged at all if it hadn't been for the Old Man and his like. The brutes might still have existed, but without becoming visible. But *could* they have existed if they were never seen?

Was I trying to hold the Old Man responsible for the wolves' existence? Yes, in a way. But then if no one had conjured them out of their world of invisible violence, if no one had identified them, it would have been impossible to hunt them down.

But once he'd been killed by the surging power of the wolves, the father figure was definitely dead. However much I admired him as he had been before—a father who played dead in order to show up more clearly the passion of the living—I knew now that the world had changed. In Santa Varvara they had killed the "dead" father. Was the Old Man the last of them? All that remained were such as Vespasian. But it's hard to be a man when you're neither child nor youth nor parent. When there's no father, the wolves prowl, metamorphoses multiply and cancel one another out, canine jaws invade the fashionable parts of town, and the suburbs too. But who sees them? Why, the detectives, male or female: sardonic and hunted disciples of the "dead" father, who wait for dark to laugh alone over their whisky, then try to work out who the lake murderer was, and fall asleep zapping the television, where one image is followed by another and metamorphoses never cease.

5

Where do detectives come from? Judging by my own experience, you become a detective when, having no place of your own, you appoint yourself an ambassador of the law and spend your life trying to solve a mystery that is really a murder.

"What does it mean, I wonder—being an ambassador?" (My

mother's questions were always protests disguised as curiosity. But why did she bother, and for whose benefit? We were all quite conscious of being reproached.) "You're away from home—that's the essence of the matter. You represent a kind of mirage, someone who's never there —the Holy Ghost, probably." And a detective may be a degraded, compromised, even corrupt version of the kind of go-between whose nobler aspect is embodied in an ambassador.

We were out of place everywhere: uprooted in Santa Varvara, expatriates in Paris, just passing through in both. Nomads on a mission by definition impossible. Feeling myself at a distance from everyone and everything everywhere, I became mistrustful: people and objects alike seemed to me unhinged, unnatural, deceitful, hypocritical. In short, suspect. And although I saw myself too as entrusted with a mission, I didn't identify with the invisible force that had made us all its representatives. Anyhow, did it really exist, that distant chimera from which Father received instructions and a perfectly tangible salary, but that for my own generation was merely an abstract principle—at best a memory, at worst a symbol of the fact that I didn't belong to the community of Santa Varvara, the community of the wolves, any community at all.

A lot of individuals gathered together generate their own carapace, the kind of biological glue secreted by any tribe of animals. It frightened me. But I learned to penetrate the barrier by pretending to enter into their skins and their ways, pretending to become one of them. I experienced Santa Varvara from within, but turned myself inside out like a glove in order to see and hear it as from a distance. This oscillation might be called a kind of justice: it wasn't respect for good itself, but it was reversible space, the essence of ambassadorship, of mission—a to-ing and fro-ing between compromise and revelation. Father, like the Old Man, had a horror of detectives: he suspected them of being in league with the police, who in Santa Varvara were all too plainly related to the wolves. I neither wanted nor dared to discuss this suspicion with him, though I thought it mistaken: he'd never read any detective stories and knew nothing about the underworld. Anyhow, he would never have accepted the possibility that his own vocation might have inspired a daughter of his to become a sleuth . . .

On the marquetry top of the Louis Quinze escritoire there stood a Dresden china fruit bowl guarded by a marquis and his marquise, bowing and curtsying prettily to one another. The piece was made of fine, resonant porcelain that might have been taken for an enormous white diamond if it hadn't been so fragile. When it was full of peaches, grapes or apples, it gave out the kind of delicate perfume that can fill the musty austerity of a library with mouthwatering dreams of orchards. No one dared touch the fruit for fear of shattering the fruit bowl's classical harmony; little girls aren't always hungry, anyway. Nonetheless, the peaches, the bunches of grapes, and the apples used somehow to dwindle mysteriously, though the bowl was never left empty. Whoever hankered after the fruit must have been afraid to expose the inside of the bowl, which was white, dotted with garlands of scarlet flowers. So the small, lordly dish always contained at least two apples. In the languishing hours of the afternoon the smell of them would combine with the scent of ink and old leather to produce an aroma as enticing—to me, at any rate—as the smell of someone cooking crème caramel. Then all of a sudden the marquise disappeared too.

There were no two ways about it: there must be a thief around. For two whole nights my brain, protected by a semblance of sleep, screened computerized tables showing every logical possibility: friends of the family, my father's colleagues, the Old Man himself (why not?), our schoolmates, the cleaning lady, and of course the mailman—computers have no scruples. Finally, I went down to breakfast, hungry as a hunter and revolving in my mind the name of the culprit. The only person I told was my father. The guilty party was a schoolfriend of mine, a plump, fair-haired little girl with whom I'd grown so friendly I'd allowed her to trespass on the forbidden ground of the ambassador's study. She wasn't as standoffish as Alba Ram, and didn't share her worship of the twelve Caesars; nor did she show the restrained intelligence that Alba manifested as a newcomer coming from the provinces as well as from a good family. I'd gone so far as to identify myself with that chubby little blonde with white socks and a big bow in her hair. And having let her usurp my place, I also put myself in hers, and guessed that she was jealous, and that her jealousy not only made her hungry but also made her covet my little Dresden marquise. She didn't want to possess the precious statuette in order to worship it—anyone might have spotted it then, even if she kept it hidden in the pocket of her shorts. No, she only wanted the marquise in order to kill her: to smash her to powder and pull the plug on her.

"You'd make a good detective," my father said, after we'd decided not to tell anyone else. But he soon changed his tune. "You discovered the crime and the criminal because you worked it all out faster than the rest of us. So concentrate on your math!"

But alas, I didn't become a scientist. I didn't have enough perseverance. All I had was the adaptability and the nerve to put myself in someone else's place. I didn't ask the little thief round to our house any more. But one day at school I did tell her my theory about the marquise having been murdered, ground to dust, and flushed down the toilet. She blushed and ran out into the playground. From then on I grew closer to Alba, and she became my best friend. I can still work things out faster than other people. At least, I try to.

6

Writing about the lives and manners of the people I knew, whether I did so inoffensively or arrogantly, might have led me to take a more distant stand and go in for biography. Many people prefer to set aside the modest incidents of their own lives and deal with the hallowed matter of History: the fantasies of Faust, Ulysses, Don Juan, Christ, Abraham, or the Wandering Jew, to name but a few, not to mention the heroes of art, literature, and science, so infinitely more significant and worthy of attention than a writer's own unremarkable experience. Besides, we've already gone on so much about ourselves that there isn't much left to be said on the subject but tedious platitudes; whereas the passing show goes by faster and faster, and the news or a game show on TV is much more amusing than the flattering versions we construct of the vagaries of our own minds and hearts. Rehashing glorious pages on past idols and rearranging the exhibits in their museums is infinitely more entertaining than picking forever at our own petty wounds.

Of course, the virtuosi of literature have already chosen the better part, and I'm the first to provide myself with their masterpieces when I take off for the investigations, crises, and other humanitarian missions my editor assigns me—preferably in some godforsaken hole at the back of beyond where I need supplies of genius and beauty in order to survive.

It won't be long now till women are the only ones who still

believe in the personal, still think—for women know how very ordinary they are themselves—that an ordinary individual may be of interest. So I go on telling you about my whims and fancies because, like the Professor, I persist in thinking that *quodlibet ens* means not "no matter what being" but "a being that matters, no matter what."

Father mattered to me, no matter what, despite the indifference we both affected. I suppose our wills kept up a reciprocal relationship. *Libet*, the Professor insisted, refers to our mutual desire for one another's ordinary virtues. "X is such that he belongs to Y." Chrysippus liked to deduce moral values from this logical commonplace. Father's virtue stopped short at the brink of utterance: for me, his virtue consisted in being an X who was such . . . In not belonging to the category of fathers in general, of ambassadors, foreigners, Santa Barbarians, Frenchmen, friends, or enemies of the Professor, or any other classification whatsoever, human, inhuman, or superhuman. His virtue consisted in being *tel quel*—"as he was"—and in being content to appear as such, just as he was, and therefore thinkable and lovable by others who were the same as he, other ordinary beings. By me, for example, who am a Y to his X, and so appear to him in all my own ordinariness.

That's how we are. That's all. Exposed for all to see in our manners, our ways; produced by them. And now my memory is trying to retrace the *maniérism*, the outflow that reflected us. The kind of detail that comes back to me, Father—a smoky train, a bedroom, a Greeting to the Sun—is not your dwelling place. You didn't bequeath me either *manentia* or *mansio*; you left me neither home nor mansion. Nor, in my random recollections, do I find any trace of *manus*, the hand of power, the martial authority of *vir* over *mulier*, man over woman; nor of the hand as instrument of struggle and labor, of legal, military, or technical skill. No—my inner jigsaw puzzle, made up of bits of affect, adds up to just an outpouring, *manare*, a flowing forth of your ordinary peculiarities, and of my own, in which you live on as you are. You are, we are, completely ordinary; examples of the being that does not belong to us and yet with which, by making use of it in our own ordinary manner, we make ourselves happy. Being created by one's own manner is the only happiness possible. It is the happiness of simple folk, of ordinary people.

Let someone else have the pleasure of recreating the Noah's Ark of past geniuses and masterpieces, and find the strength to produce his own masterpiece. As for me, I'm in Santa Varvara, the now-famous city where men and women have become indistinguishable from wolves through despising the very thing whose memory I'm trying to preserve: the *quodlibet*, the being that matters no matter what. I kindle my feelings through minute details, meaningless dreams, insensate crimes; I gather up the quodlibets, the quips of ordinary loves. Father and the Old Man both had the simplicity of ordinary men, no matter who, and that was why they mattered, no matter what. Yes, amid the darkness of great men, my light, my argument is based on the *principium individuationis*, the principle of individuation. And that's what would need to be saved if ever there were another Noah's Ark, since it was by its abolition that Santa Varvara set out on the downward path. Yes, what needs preserving is the principle of individuation, the *quodlibet*, the Old Man, and my father.

The only way I could mourn was by making their ordinariness seem lovable to you. I plead for a truce in our fascination with murder, though I haven't forgotten about it and promise to get back to it in due course. But for the time being, try to remember there is an X who exists just as he shows himself to you: irritating, thinkable, lovable.

⌐ 8. Men of Sorrow

1

"THE PROFESSOR suffers because he was born an orphan. There's no getting away from it." (Father had read Freud.)

The Old Man's father was killed in the war, I don't know which war, but what does it matter—one of those wars that are pointless when viewed from outer space, but at the same time indispensable to History and miserable for the families involved. Septicius Clarus's mother died in childbirth. "She gave him life at the same time as she herself died in order to rejoin her husband." (The relations went straight to the point.) I personally think she'd had enough of her five brats and the huge fields of sunflowers and maize, which she couldn't cope with, which everyone else coveted, and which they finally stole from her.

And so the Old Man was, in a manner of speaking, born. A friend of the family, a widow, adopted him. She loved him like a son, and, I suspect, like a lover too, for the Professor had the fineness of feeling you find in most little boys who've been brought up among older women. But he lived as if he'd always known that his body was the grave of two dead people. His otherworldly smile was due to the fact that he thought of himself as already belonging to another world. And though he never spoke of it, he made himself sick and silent with an otherworldly suffering completely beyond the ken of the wolves.

I find myself wondering if he didn't share that suffering with God. People lost no time in offering him the usual gift proposed to orphans, the pride of those in distress: the proposition that "God is love." But he didn't bite. He was more at home with Ovid in exile and the morbid songs of Tibullus, lover of Delia: a world of change and metamorphosis in which the ancient gods aroused sordid passions and in which a new Messiah was scarcely credible. He loved to read the books written in that period of transition, and to discuss its ideas, myths, and morals.

Yet he didn't reject the God who was his one and only inheritance. He even, unobtrusively, turned Him into his secret home: for he had no other, apart from his Latin books. Moreover, after his daughters had gone away and his wife was dead, the only family he had left were his students: he said they brought him consolation and fulfillment. Alba's bronze tresses done up into a chignon; the logical tricks of Chrysippus, the genius of the class; my own determination to neglect ordinary subjects and go off at some improbable tangent. All this amused him, and he would urge us on: "Go on, go on—I want you to go further! Show me what comes next!" But to tell the truth we weren't up to much, we couldn't help him. It was he who helped us—the people of Santa Varvara, I mean.

So he lived with God, and no one was ever so faithful to a God from whom he'd received and of whom he asked nothing. All he did was thank Him. But for what, for God's sake? He really had nothing to thank Him for. Unless perhaps for *being*, for being afflicted and not speaking about it, even to God? That's it, that's what he was saying: thank you for letting me be able to suffer and say nothing, even to God. And also, thank you for letting Alba and Stephie guess, perhaps. Though they didn't guess till after he was dead.

2

He'd torn himself away from his village, and even from his adoptive mother—I suppose his was the kind of exile people embark on in a moment of wild aberration and without thinking of the risk—to live the life of a migrant, which continued uninterrupted until his dubious death in the military hospital. Of course, he liked to rove around Santa Varvara's various landscapes, whether fertile or barren; to see himself as a mountaineer or a frog-man; to snuff up the scent of dead leaves in the fall; to go cross-country skiing across remote border plateaux. But his real journey was among books. Septicius Clarus's mother having died young, he replaced his mother tongue with a passion for a dead language, and by breathing new life into Latin tomes that his contemporaries now neglected, rejected, or knew nothing about, he embarked on a countdown that he regarded as having a great future. Septicius, fleeing from the present of the wolves to the past of the Romans in the expectation of changes he himself might dream of but would never live to see, was a nomad. When barbarism reigns, the only form of civilization may be migration, a nomadism based on the strange ability some people possess of never identifying with "themselves" or "here" or "now." The power to be always finding other places without losing their minds.

"Make up your mind, old boy," Vespasian would snap, over tea in the apartment over Gulliver's wife's fountain. "We only live once—with our own contemporaries, in our own age. But you—where are you? In what time? What place? I'll tell you if you like! It's true a woman like Alba may find your daydreams attractive. But if you want my sincere opinion, you are utterly irresponsible. No offense meant, Clarus, but you're a shirker, and that's all there is to it."

The Old Man didn't care to argue, especially with Vespasian, but, far from being nonexistent, as the younger man had alleged, his principles were absolutely firm and unwavering. He had made a conscious decision to be a nomad, not to be fixed in any one place, to avoid people who settled down and were sure of themselves and of the here and the now. Travel wasn't merely a criticism or a sign of crisis. It was a choice, an option, an attitude: a quest for what is to be that sets out from what has been, without a fixed plan but free to open up all kinds of avenues. For example, the avenues of memory, which once made Santa Varvara one of the capitals of metamorphosis, as Ovid and Tibullus and even Suetonius could confirm. Whereas now the same city was merely the sinister scene of dreadful transmogrifications, though these might one day be succeeded by something better.

"Go away, Alba—go away! Do as I do—I'm always on the move. Your Vespasian is right on that score."

But Alba couldn't move. She was rooted to the spot, like a tree, like a stone.

She tried, perhaps. But if so, she tried in vain.

Now that he'd made his last journey and would never again, ironically and paternally, admire me going off with my trunks and my typewriter to catch a plane, I wondered whether it was-n't the passion for departure, the love of change, the craze for always being somewhere else, that people, with characteristic haste and conformism, called the Professor's "faith."

3

So perhaps God is the invisible entity that sets a dis-tance between us and our passions: an interval we experience as pride.

Did the Old Man exhibit that minimal but noble fragment of divinity because the wolves were everywhere, devouring our bread and our words? Septicius Clarus transformed his anguish into the humility of a faith that was hidden but not in the least craven. On the contrary, he was soberly and stubbornly inde-pendent.

He didn't talk about it, though—as I've already said, he spoke only of Ovid and Tibullus. Song was his way of giving himself to his God. When he listened, his eyes widened and filled with bluish light. His face opened up into something beyond skin and bone, yet despite his rapture what he heard was corporeal, clear, precise. And, just as others may listen with their throats, so the Old Man sang with his fibers, his sea-sensitive retinas and eardrums. I'd seen and heard him, because Father and I often went with him to the old churches where people used to go at the beginning of the invasion to escape the wolves. His voice was all hearing and sight. Its tenor flights were strict and disciplined, without either tremor or boom—pure notes, a pattern of metallic sound. Was it to make up for that asceticism and precision, such worlds away from the pathos of Italian opera, aimed at the ladies, that he infused the words themselves and his movements with emotion? Thus articulation, gesture, and sound between them wove one pure language: music flowed into words, words rose up into music. For a more eclectic music-lover that kind of structure might have seemed to hover on the brink of aridity or even the absurd. But Father admired and even imitated it: he used to sing along with Clarus. In my view, they were celebrating the marriage of discourse and music—their osmosis, the limits beyond which they are no longer separate.

Strangely enough, though Septicius Clarus meant his singing to reach us, he didn't make undue efforts to make it do so. His face and his words, both colored with emotion, were turned inwards. "He's saying his prayers," Alba would say. She was jealous at not being drawn into the mystery. Personally, I preferred to think he was mating with his God, and that this giving of himself was so total and natural, so pure and yet so physical, so indecent and yet so sexless, that it shouldn't be exposed to voyeurs. Either the whole world ought to be like him—open, jubilant, modest—or else all the rest of us should disappear, overwhelmed with shame at not being up to his fineness and vibrancy. I'd have liked to join him, *be* him, tremble with that intellected voice in which he and his unseen principle were one. But I couldn't sing.

So sometimes I would start to laugh. A diabolical counterpart to his angelism. I was shattered by my own inability to share that surreptitious, burning eroticism, and felt even more worthless and rejected than before. "It's her age." (My mother.) The Professor, like my father, would forgive me, though he was visibly upset. And then he would continue with his favorite song, in which the hero, about to be beheaded, asked to have his hair and his shirt washed so that he might be all clean and airy when he met his Maker. My nerves would now turn my giggles to hysteria: I felt like crying. And I used to slink out of the room, convinced once and for all that I was incapable of God.

4

My father, though, would linger with the Professor amid old churches and Roman ruins dating back to the first century B.C., perhaps even the third or fourth. The two men grew so inseparable that people often mixed them up. In the early days of the invasion those secret places served as places of refuge. Until the wolves found their way there. There'd been leaks; someone had given us away. "Monsieur Delacour's always with Septicius Clarus—Monsieur Delacour goes to church."

The persecution extended even to us, the children. Father soon became persona non grata, and the whole family had to leave Santa Varvara. This was fortunate for us, but not for the Professor, left all alone but for Alba and Chrysippus.

Meanwhile, though I was only a child, I'd come to know the atmosphere that reigned in Santa Varvara, and I never forgot it.

My father had learned to act as if his isolation, which was really a humiliation, were a kind of distinction: he went with head held high; his eyes, though taking in the wretched country's troubles, were so bright he seemed to be always smiling. Wasn't misfortune made to be overcome? But though, for himself, he treated it all as a cross he had to bear, he broke down when the disgrace began to affect Vicky and me. His dismay wasn't visible from the outside. ("Life's a battle, Stephie Delacour," he'd say, "and you might as well know it. But good losers bide their time and prepare their comeback.") But I could sense it eating him up from within like an ulcer, making his cheeks go sallow and his hands tremble.

I can still remember the day I threw my ball through a

neighbor's window. Nothing unusual about that. Except that
the old witch emerged, without her broom, and spitting
insults: "Blah blah blah . . . morals . . . the community . . . But
of course you don't know anything about all that! Your father's
turned into a churchgoer, so I suppose he fills your head with
fine words—but never a word about respecting other people's
property!" For as I'd soon find out, despite their apparent
enthusiasm for the "community" the citizens of Santa Varvara, like people everywhere else, were interested only in property. But to own, to have, made you an accomplice of the
wolves, whom you regarded as the guardians of your possessions when in fact they were devouring you.

"She lives with the wolves, so she's getting to be like them,"
was the Professor's comment.

Father never mentioned God to us: the subject wasn't on the
school curriculum in Santa Varvara, and he didn't want to
upset his daughters or depart too far from diplomatic discretion. But everyone knew by now that he joined in the singing
when he went to mass with the Professor, and that this was a
far from blameless act.

"Stephie's very good in every subject. We must put her
name down for the English high school." (Mother was always
practical.)

So they duly applied, but Father was skeptical. There was no
reply, and after a certain amount of time had gone by the explanation was obvious. Then, without saying anything to me, my
darling father made a further effort: he thought he was putting
up a fight, though he was merely adding to his humiliation. He
wrote to the then President of Santa Varvara—I don't remember his name, something like Vespasian, I seem to recall, but
I'm probably wrong, and what's the difference?—wrote a letter
of protest, asking on what grounds our application had been
rejected. Unfortunately it was I who picked up the answer

from the President whose name was something like Vespasian (I still can't remember it, and with good reason).

But I'll always remember that great big mailbox. Father and the Old Man must have found it in some sacristy: the front had holes in the shape of crosses all over it; it was meant to shield the flames of candles burning during prayers. It was a very unusual mailbox, quite different from all the others in the gray concrete apartment building we lived in in the new town. I found the letter from the President—let's call him President Vespasian—with the appropriate inscription on the envelope, and couldn't resist the temptation. "Comrade Ambassador . . . your daughter . . . you are not a member of the Party . . . and, let me remind you, you are a believer and very involved with certain local believers . . . You will agree that this, quite objectively, places you among the enemies of Santa Varvara . . . I am amazed you should have thought your daughter worthy of such a distinguished establishment . . . can only reiterate our categorical refusal."

I sealed the letter up again and said nothing. Neither did my father. But he was very pale that evening, suffering with his ulcer.

"It's the spring—it always plays up in the spring." (My mother had an answer for everything.) But I knew very well what spring it was. I tried to tell him, just with my eyes, that I knew everything and didn't hold it against him. It seemed to me he'd guessed. He shut himself up in his pride, and was in pain for the rest of the week.

5

I've never seen any other man with a finger like the Professor's. The middle finger on his right hand. The top joint was rounded and without a nail—just a tobacco-colored curve sprouting from the base of what might have been a nail. It was as if the animal nature that exists in everyone—surviving in apparently harmless form in the fingernails, to all intents and purposes useless, which women file and varnish as if to conceal some obscene secret—had been partially overcome in the Old Man. Was he a mutant, a saint who'd managed to rid himself of savagery? "Unless the opposite is true," I would think when he scolded me (for Septicius was extremely exacting, and could get very angry). "He may be a cruel wild beast, a beast of prey. His maimed fingernail is really an eagle's beak, a tiger's claw, the barbarous essence he hides beneath Gregorian chant."

Septicius himself told an amusing story to account for this anomaly. He recounted the "anecdote" with relish, and as we listened we would alternate between love and hate, via the smug condescension that's often bestowed on the confidences of the elderly. He was a bold child, and when he was still getting about on all fours he escaped from his adoptive mother, who'd taken him to a children's circus in Santa Varvara, and crawled over to the platform where a tiger was on display. And the wicked beast had pounced on the child's hand and started to gnaw the finger before the animal's keepers could come to the rescue and prevent it from gobbling up the small boy altogether.

"I didn't feel anything, though they told me my mother fainted," Scholasticus would say, smiling, "but ever since then I've always been able to scent out wild animals, including wolves as well as tigers."

It didn't sound very plausible. Alba would grow impatient, Vicky thought the Old Man was losing his marbles. But I was proud of having a Professor who was both angel and beast. "A case of wearing one's castration on one's sleeve," Vespasian explained some time later, when he'd started courting Alba and was told the story confidentially, as between friends.

Perhaps. It might well be, as Vespasian suggested, that the
story was the Old Man's way of reminding himself of his vul-
nerability without dwelling on it all the time. The mythical
wound might be a kind of pagan circumcision, but visible and
thus quite real. "It was cut off and so I'm not completely unim-
paired." After that, all Septicius's actions seemed to have the
battered and fragile simplicity of the innocent.

6

They're so muddled and blurred and foreshortened—
what do my memories of the Old Man really amount to? Initials merging into the memory of my father. Death mingles the
ghosts of the two accomplices as in a dream. Where does one
end and the other begin? Once upon a time there was a man
who was against the wolves . . .

Septicius Clarus used his reverence for Rome as a vehicle for
oblique criticism of our own society. My father, on the other
hand, while eschewing positive precepts, boldly drew attention to whatever struck him as wrong. I don't know which of
the two was the more disillusioned.

We knew another family, the Aguilars, with seven sons, all
students and sportsmen driven by their father's ambition. No
pleasure was allowed to show its nose, no perception, no feeling, no dream—whether it arose from sailing, walking, cycling,
or even strolling through the fields or lying on the grass beside
our holiday tents and staring up at the sky—without the
Aguilars translating everything into figures. I'd be letting
myself dissolve in the waves. "Who won?" the father of the
Aguilars would demand. "I did it in two minutes and thirty-
four seconds!" one of the sons would yell in triumph. "I stayed
under for ninety seconds without breathing!" claimed another.

"I got there in one minute and twenty-five seconds," a third would announce, trumping all the others.

Above our sleepy, faintly amorous heads there stretched a starry sky. "Can you see the Pole Star? And the Great Bear, just next to it? Got it? And Stephie—what's that constellation on the left? You don't know? You don't know much, do you? What a dope!" I was taken aback, but anyhow I didn't really like him.

"Father, Vicky beat me at chess!" the youngest Aguilar boy finally admitted, much put out by this Waterloo. "Well, play her again and win!" ordered the head of the family.

"What's the matter with them?" I asked one day.

"They don't have any feelings or any thoughts—only figures and balance sheets," my father explained, trying to make light of our defeats. I presume the Aguilars have all succeeded in life since, as far as figures and balance sheets are concerned.

Yesterday one of those hyperefficient sons recognized me in the *Oasis* and said to me, point-blank, after all those years when we hadn't set eyes on one another: "I'm making money hand over fist out of these Santa Varvara hicks! A turnover of forty million a month! Not bad, eh?"

I didn't ask him what his business was. Packaging, soap, drugs, arms? It made no difference. Aguilar had become indistinguishable from his balance sheet long ago, and hadn't noticed the wolves. The Professor would have said he'd turned into one of them. Because he was entirely incapable of any kind of relaxation or distraction. Completely immune to poetry.

7

I can see a mother-of-pearl sunset from Alba's apartment building, overlooking Santa Varvara. It reminds me of a cloud I once saw against the volcanic landscape of Fort-de-

France in Martinique. White or gold, I don't remember, opaque but iridescent, a touch of artifice floating over all that nature full of water, heat, and chance. The exact opposite of Santa Varvara. I never had the chance to tell him about it. I'd thought of taking him there, treating him to a trip to my island refuge. But I didn't say anything about it. He'd probably have refused, anyway. And was I really serious about it? For him it was enough to know I was happy somewhere in the world. Then he'd transport himself there in his imagination, enjoying everything as if he were me. A postcard was enough for him. Not even that—the mere idea of my going somewhere made him dream in colors and tastes.

After the invasion began, and the wolves and the famine, if anyone gave him a chocolate he'd save it up for me in his pocket instead of eating it himself. "It tastes sweeter to me when you eat it, my darling," he'd say. I would be sulking and turning up my nose. I didn't like sweets, I didn't like eating at all. What an idea—saving up bits of food! The fad of a silly old man.

I couldn't get him out of the military hospital or take him to be operated on in Paris. He always outdid me in courtesy and fineness of feeling. So he, with his muted passion, will never see that cloud over those mountains shamelessly bare as the breasts of the young Creole women. It cut across the sea, giving depth to the sky. Tonight the sky is yellow and silky, like the cloak of an Italian page.

Yes, I know—he had thousands of visions of his own, different visions, more exciting to him than my dreams of bare-bosomed Creole girls and Renaissance palettes. But he'll never see that cloud, never feel this tenderness, never be able to come to that island, my Candide's garden. And it's my fault. I didn't do anything for the Old Man. It's foolish to regret acts of generosity never performed. But I can't help weeping the unrelieving tears that mourn missed understandings.

8

The fine but vivid memory of winter, its whirling flakes almost blotting out the present morning, is clearer than the warm recollections of summer, which veil the mind rather than the eye so that my father is always present, glowing like the sea in the light of a July sun. My images of Santa Varvara in winter are bright but lonely, inducing a feeling of emptiness. It must be the cold reaching out to my skin and bones from the far-off days when my father and Septicius used to pull me in a sledge around the frozen lake in the park, or through the snowy hills that enclosed with firs and rumors of wolves the unremarkable town that had come to be the setting of my childhood. The streetcar would stop halfway to the mountains, not far from a royal palace converted into a youth center. (In Santa Varvara, as everywhere else, people attached great importance to centers and the younger generation when they wanted to forget the wolves or pretend they didn't exist.) I would get off the bus, my fingers, toes, and nose all tingling with cold, arrange my balaclava, and install myself in the sled, a handmade affair that my father and the Old Man would take turns pulling across the virgin snow. I shouted with laughter whenever it went too fast, skidded and overturned, tipping me out into the drifts and covering me with a powdering of white that melted as soon as we got home and I was in the warm.

Such images, so often experienced, enjoyed, or endured in the past, and still haunting my words and dreamed of deep down in the cells of my brain and body, have paled into oblivion. Only fragments remain, but fragments as finely carved as frost on the windows of houses in winter.

The bus leaves behind the misty hollow in which the city of Santa Varvara crouches, and climbs on up towards the airy summit. Father's silhouette rises out of the fog that stretches back to the town; he seems to be emerging above the clouds. A squirrel shakes the branches of a fir tree as we pass underneath, and a lump of snow falls down on to the tassel of my cap. Muffled up as I am, I can hear Septicius speaking, but can't understand what he says, or my Father's lengthy reply. I snuggle down inside my scarf. They've forgotten me, the slow movement of the sled is making me sleepy, but I'm cold, and there are shadows moving about among the leafless bushes. Wolves?

I receive a telegram. A death. The name is illegible. Something tells me it's Father. The words are blurred, as if by a melting snowflake, but the initials look like an S and a C. The Professor. The sled overturns, but no one picks me up. It goes on snowing, falling and falling on top of me, and I'm cold. My feet are frozen, my hair too, the snow is like numbingly icy water seeping into my bones, into my socks and gloves, into all the wraps that are supposed to keep out the cold. It's like being in a refrigerator; I'm a corpse. And there's no one there except those hostile shadows again, the wolves among the bushes. I can feel nothing but the sense of ultimate defeat imparted by death. Nothing except perhaps the sensation of winter, which was written into my infant cells back in the mists of time and makes its way, through words, into my memory and my dreams, dropping icy flakes into the warm bed. Sleep loses its comfort; it starts to thaw, melting at the touch of a thought, at a terror, at wakening. Someone is no more. Someone is cold and dead.

Mourning is memory, weeping and catching its breath at the thought of winters past.

9

He'd been asleep in the wind, on the beach, still rather distraught after escaping from Santa Varvara, but glad to be on the other side of the world. "What's this? Where has the sea disappeared to? Am I dreaming?" As a good son of the Mediterranean, he was pretending to be surprised at the height of the tides, the power of the moon. As was his habit, he made fun of himself as a way of thanking me for coming with him.

"It looks as though there's been a cosmic disaster! I know it's only temporary, but I can't help being scared. I feel like the last human being watching the earth drying up in some ecological catastrophe and about to vanish from the universe. He'd never believe it might all start up again in another million years; or rather, he wouldn't care whether it did or not. Well, I'm just like that poor fellow. I find it hard to believe the tide will ever come in again."

My father tended to the apocalyptic. He'd seen so many falls and crashes and low tides in his lifetime that he was always looking out for signs of the end of the world. But he was never really worried; in fact he was so unruffled he seemed almost to look forward to disaster. But ever since Santa Varvara he'd kept his presentiments to himself, his only visible attitude a kind of shy enthusiasm. In general it's impossible for someone to be enthusiastic and reticent at the same time. But he managed it because he didn't believe in anything that might happen. It was all a matter of indifference to him. But he believed in things for me.

For him, it was low tide everywhere and forever. "All things considered, you know, politics is pretty low." But I, Stephie Delacour, was there, he said, to stir up the ebb and flow, and perhaps to get some happiness out of it one of these days. You never knew; there might be a chance.

It was scarcely credible. Why me? No reason at all. Wasn't I programmed for low tide too: to contemplate the mud, to be a part of it? But no—come, come! Stephie wasn't like all the rest, she'd come through, she'd go far . . . What a hope!

But he had a reason: he loved me. It was a reason so unassuming it made the chivalrous, protective expression on his face unbearable to contemplate. His exquisite delicacy troubled me: I wondered if he wasn't weak, despite his eccentricities, an ambassador. Had he really got the courage of his convictions, this diplomat always ready to walk away if he found he was dealing with someone dim or aggressive or coarse?

Like the Professor, he had to die for me to see those mild expressions of his again. I used to dismiss snapshots of him, snapshots like this one, as trivial glimpses of a Quakerlike ordinariness. But that wasn't it at all. He was really exposing himself, with trusting gentleness, with a kind of shattered tension of eye and skin, in permanent prayer.

But beneath the overt supplication there was a deep, subcutaneous disillusion that hinted at indelible pain. He was always being hurt, though no one saw it except the Professor: his friend, his double. I myself knew nothing about it. I took him for a casualty in search of an impossible priesthood; a troubled spirit whom the post as ambassador to Santa Varvara had really suited down to the ground.

Affliction turns hope to courtesy. Bitterness and ambition disappear, and the face that the man of sorrow turns toward me holds both welcome and mystery. The sort of thing to make a child curious, perhaps even clever. For while happiness invites no questions, suffering makes you wonder.

With his basketful of oysters, his rubber boots frosted with salt from the sea, his knives and hammers and other fishing tackle sticking out of the pocket of his oilskin, he radiates the joys of low tide, of our gathering oysters together amid the sandy furrows. He merges into the rising wind from the sea. He doesn't know whom to thank for this blessing—the moon, or God, or me.

I look at the photograph more closely. The suffering is still there, but no one has put a name to it. It's a suffering that he was able to forget, which I hope he was able to give up altogether. For he didn't need much. A fishing trip, a child's hand in his, and his happiness would be transformed into chivalry: he was congratulating the sand and the oysters for being there. For him, pleasure had come to mean being suspended briefly out of the reach of pain.

~ 9. Where's the Crime?

1

EVERYONE HAS a mother tongue. I got mine from my father. From the songs he sang and the poems he recited to me that I quickly learned by heart, from his stories and nursery rhymes, from his accounts of all the books he read—novels, histories, biographies—especially in order to tell us about them.

He backed up the language itself with his eyes, wide-open with some fathomless meaning, showing me that speech wasn't merely a part of everyday life but had an independent existence that moved in light and air and space, and was free.

Fortunately my mother was there to give words back their down-to-earth meaning: salt, bread, water, milk, washing, ironing, sewing. All the things we live by, lack, or use. Still, speech is a fact and not a dream, and because it's so close to things it doesn't even strike us as arbitrary. That kind of language was self-evident, and thus natural, unique, absolute: in short—Mother was sure of it—it was one's mother tongue.

But because for my father everything was miraculous, belonging to the weightlessness beyond pain that was his very life, I was certain the discourse that linked the two of us together must be artificial: something that made us alien to the world around us, dreaming, rambling, always alone and yet in tune with one another. If it hadn't been for Mother, we might have been in danger of going off the rails altogether—the Professor, my father, and I. Thanks to her, it was clear that this special speech of ours was only a game, a permissible curiosity.

And that was how I went on, through my father, to foreign languages, including algebra, Russian, English, Chinese—not forgetting the first of them, which was Santa Varvarian. With the result that Stephie Delacour can travel around the world in every language, telling crazy stories everywhere without feeling she's translating (or betraying).

The whole range of artifices was henceforth available to me. Father had passed on to me his God, the same as the Professor's, in the logical form of an infinity of languages. He opened up that galaxy to me as if foreign words were going to play the part of seraphim for me, flocks of angels helping me soar through secret skies. Did he ever suspect this celestial teaching of his would drive me away for good, from him and the Professor and all the rest, from places, bodies, and roots? Perhaps not.

Unless of course he'd set his own body, place, and roots aside. Maybe he wasn't interested in them; maybe he'd dissolved the pain they caused him in the otherworldiness of his singing and the shy delicacy that was always apologizing for being there.

In bestowing on me the gift of tongues, my diplomat father

kept me away from his grave. But he brought me nearer to what I've called his weightlessness: his other world, that midway state, half sad, half happy, which made him a stranger everywhere, a man apart.

I don't think he knew what he was doing, at least in the beginning. But toward the end of his life, whenever he saw me packing my bags for my umpteenth trip as a reporter, his visionary eyes would fill with laughter. "To think I've handed down to you a permanent Flight out of Egypt! The only worthwhile thing I've done in my whole life will have been snatching my daughters from the jaws of hell!"

Hell—what's that? Santa Varvara? Original sin? The absence of infinity?

2

I didn't really feel I was sharing my thoughts, my joys, and my sorrows with him. Father and daughter impose a certain reticence upon themselves, if resentment doesn't fossilize their passions altogether. But since his death I've noticed I don't communicate with anyone any more. Logically speaking, that means I must have communicated with someone once. But with whom, if not with him?

Communicate—another empty word. I once had a lover who got his wife to write to him every day when he went away with me on vacation. Having put the daily missive away in the pocket of his shorts, he would stroke my legs and feet with such skill and abandon it was enough to give pleasure to the tree trunks all around us. "You can love someone through the soles of their feet," he'd say, patting the guardian letter in his back pocket. I was prepared to believe him, and stretched out sensual toes toward the other woman's epistle.

We betray because proofs of love are not enough for us: we cancel them out as fast as we give them, destroying such meager reasons as our partners have managed to dig up for having anything to do with us.

But Father loved like a flower open to the blessing of dawn-warmed dew; not judging, not calculating, not asking anything. In that limitless expectation, he was neither subject nor object. He was an offering. I suppose I'm praising a man I confuse with his love, or with my own. The beginnings of eulogy are to be found in funeral orations. The decorating of corpses. How absurd. He doesn't need it. I consign my eulogy to the dust, his dust, out of which grows a flower in ecstasy.

3

The Professor, like my father, was far from earthy. The toil of Adam left him cold. When I took up gardening and he saw me plunging my fingers into the rich soil, pulling up weeds, planting seeds, snuffing up the smell of sap and honey that rises up when you water the garden, he would throw up his hands in astonishment, as if I were the reincarnation of some not merely forgotten but utterly impossible ancestor. But, to please me, he would tirelessly water the element that one day would receive him. I could see that thought didn't occur to him, though: he was just joining in the game I played in the intervals of my expeditions to the four corners of the world. He toyed with the clay in order to tend me: to feed me, wash me, make me beautiful. But his eyes were elsewhere: in the wind and in the sky.

Now that the people of Santa Varvara have incinerated him, I tell myself that, after all, fire suits him better than earth. But I'll never forgive the wolves for refusing him the right of burial. "We don't have graves any more in Santa Varvara," declared Vespasian, pooh-poohing what he considered an anachronistic ritual. Then he added: "Only atheists will be allowed to have mausoleums in future!" Such idiocy left me speechless.

And so they burned him, and I shrank, became a lump of basalt, an incurable anguish. The wolves will never succeed in devouring the quintessence of endurance and resistance that crime reduces us to, if it doesn't completely destroy us. I shall survive their flames as if I were a stone.

But they have turned him to ashes, and now I can hang him up in the air if I want to, scatter him over water or in the sky, or even bury him underneath my flowers. All right—earth wasn't his element. Fire suits him better: he was always burning his pain into images. His singing, his self-effacement, and the modesty in his eyes were a permanent furnace. The wolves' ferocity finally overcame their stupidity: it was as if the malice of men and wolves was transmuted into the comprehension of a superhuman, a cosmic truth. His ashes were the ultimate symbol of his fragmented being, the way he had atomized himself and invested the parts in missions, visions, and embassies.

I too have my apparitions. There's one image obsessing me at the moment. The little incense-smelling church turns into a dark engraving. A recumbent effigy, lying on a tomb surrounded by a hideous crowd with heads like bats or monsters, has just written its will. The bony hand is still holding the quill, and I can read what it has written: *Nada*. Nothing. The Old Man, who not only wrote commentaries on Ovid and Tibullus but also chanted the glory of God inside the wolves' very jaws, had such a penetrating effect on everyone and everything that he brought them all face to face with their own nothingness. Now, reduced to nothing, they open their eyes and see him as he was and will remain: a man of nothing, who rejects their perversity. Crime begins when people forget to be nothing. It was that same nothing that both sickened the Professor and inspired the passion for Latin that enabled him to see and judge so clearly.

I try to console myself by imagining that the fire gave the Old Man back the violent *mal-être*, the rebellious unease that consumed him all his life. That the fierceness of the flames joined with the bursts of rage he spent his life restraining and polishing into something else. Anger was restored to him, setting him alight within now that there was no longer anyone for it to fall on. Fire ravaged and destroyed him, returned him to the void; but he wasn't there any more. He never was there: he was in my eyes and ears and in my words. For me, he didn't attain the fullness of his passion until after he died. He was just passing through, just an address he let me know about. The wolves may keep his ashes—I take away with me his words and his obsessions, his singing and his suffering: he has been transposed into me, a metamorphosis that might have amused that persistent reader of Ovid. The void entered into me together with the smile of a father who sang with pain, and I am becoming that void.

4

One of those hot Indian summer nights that dry tears that have been wept but call forth those unshed. There's always someone to tell you you mustn't weep. A mother tells her son, a daughter her aged mother, a man his wife. But to forbid the signs of sorrow in someone else is an act of hatred arising out of a long struggle against one's own humiliation: "I'm in pain myself, or not available, and so *you* mustn't cry." The weepers know nothing about the first part of this argument, but because they think the other person may have something to do with their own suffering, they bow to his scourge and stifle their lamentations, leaving their eyes stupidly empty both of tears and of succor. So eyes are dry, despair forbidden, and we are left with the dumb misery of fools. Foolish adults were once children forbidden to cry; their parents were wretched Stoics.

On this clammy night of Indian summer, my loneliness is painted on the darkness by my own empty eyes. Father said I wasn't to weep when he died. I'm sure he didn't mean it. But I can't cry anyway. Because of the wolves. There's no one to stop me; there *is* no one, period. I bore other people, and they bore me. But one doesn't weep out of boredom; one either commits suicide or goes away. *I* shall continue with my investigation.

5

It happened two years ago. Before the murders. I was accompanying the President on a trip to Santa Varvara. "You know that godforsaken hole, Stephie—you come from there, in a way. So you're going back there again tomorrow morning with the President." (My editor's idea of a joke.)

Thanks very much. I could have done without it. I was fed up with being regarded as an expert on this wretched corner of the world: no one wanted to hear about it, and it was always in some mess or other. I don't say I minded the Concorde flight, the champagne and caviar, the lightning visits, and the constant hassle over contracts always about to be signed and always being postponed; and I positively enjoyed one session in a stuffy lecture-theater full of blasé students taking advantage of the occasion to take the mickey out of their own current President. This was a kind of Vespasian who ruled them with the same mixture of stupidity and muscle as had prevailed in my childhood, made worse by the passage of time and the aging of the wolves. But the most important thing as far as I'm concerned happened after the event, and was never recorded either in the archives of the Quai d'Orsay or in the story I phoned through to my editor.

As a gesture to tolerance and human rights the visiting party went to Santa Varvara Cathedral to show everyone that, wolves or no wolves, freedom of expression came before deals on telecommunications, high-speed trains, and so on. For me, the Gregorian chant, the incense, the ancient icons, and the gilded cupolas will always have a nostalgic charm: the charm of childhood memories, which are etched on our senses of sight, hearing, and smell, and even more than words, affect our tastes—the likes and dislikes that come to us from the depths of our consciousness. In the midst of this reunion with a sensory past that I'd done my best to forget, I suddenly saw a hand waving from the balcony where the choir was seated. I recognized the Professor: and my smile was reticent as never before, so anxious was I that he should know I understood.

"Do you know that man?" (The President, a humanist, always on the alert.)

"Of course . . . It's Septicius Clarus . . . The hidden face of Santa Varvara . . . My father . . . A sweet man . . . " (I was horribly embarrassed.)

"The President would like to meet him." (The private secretary, a man of action as well as etiquette.)

What followed was rather a farce. Someone went up the right-hand staircase to the balcony. Meanwhile Septicius, having finished his stint of singing, had started to come down the left-hand staircase. They lost him, went to look for him, too late, tried again, up, down, left, right, he must have gone, no, he's praying in the crypt, yes, here we are, got him. But my President and Septicius Clarus had nothing to say to one another. Except that singing transcends prayer. Sometimes. For art is a game of God with God, which reveals only the gods—sublime but ephemeral forms.

"I didn't expect this." (The President was surprised at having to abandon contracts, statistics and Amnesty International, there, without warning, right in the middle of Santa Varvara Cathedral.)

"Compassion." (The Professor remained enigmatic, his eyes still wide with the silent incantation, the inner hymn, which I'd first encountered when I was at school. It was always there, and would suddenly come to the surface to put us in our places.)

I didn't hear what came next. Was there anything? Political visits don't usually leave time for theological debate. But in my mind's eye I shall always see that image of S.C. down in the crypt, among the medieval icons. He was glowing both with the light of the candles and from the Gregorian chant that filled his soul (he did have one), filled it to overflowing, and even managed, while that incongruous encounter lasted, to get through the Santa Varvara customs. For a few moments Septicius became the stoical citizen he'd always dreamed of being, the dazzled and Utopian agent of reconciliation. He felt as if he were being caught up into a heaven that he thought he saw open up briefly beneath the vaulted ceiling, before his very eyes, eyes all sparkling with candlelight and singing.

I had no part in it, but we were together in that dream, and I'm glad to have dreamed it with him. And now he's dead. But

I haven't said anything about his expression when he thought for a moment that the wolves had been driven out of the cathedral. Was it an illusion? Once a certain degree of bitterness has been reached, agreeable illusions become impossible; you stop expecting them. Above the tablet that the effigy is holding, with *Nada* written on it, there's now the pitying look I saw in the crypt. For a moment the Old Man caught a glimpse of the world without the wolves. Was it because of me? Had he relaxed his vigilance? Had his pity weakened him? Had the sympathy between us made him vulnerable? The illusion of being understood can make us imprudent and give the green light to murder.

One thing at least is sure: they got him. Who are "they"? Us? I got there too late. Reporters, like philosophers and owls, rise with the lark. But murders are committed in the dark, and the Old Man's pity was powerless in the night of the wolves.

6

The amount of pathos in the word *loneliness* varies according to whether it arises out of the leaving of a lover, a country, a child, or a mother . . . But death, the supreme loneliness, brings a desolation that's absolute, because there's nothing to be done about it. And to that desolation the loss of a father adds blankest anguish. The desultory affection that may have attached a daughter to her mother's husband often changes, after he is gone, into despair. She may know that despair to be odd, but just the same it affects her memory of him, a memory that is noncorporeal, consisting entirely in voice and words. But if, as sometimes happens in this sordid world, the relationship was really a tragedy of passion, the absence of the departed afflicts the daughter with a feeling of disembodied guilt that cannot even be acknowledged for what it is. Forbidden whether sublimated or realized, the love between a father and daughter is denied the delights and snares of Oedipus and Jocasta, and doomed to either the heaven of restraint or the hell of rape. And in such a case, when he dies, her mourning is encompassed with loneliness indeed. A solitude of stone.

The worst of it is that it wrings tears from me. But what is the point of weeping forever at the forbidden gates of a Law that no longer exists? It's like the wan fear of orphans, unable to hope for the impossible. It's said women don't go in for atheism because they're always in search of an illusion, namely that of a lover who will be both father and mother. But atheism may be a solution for women living in the wilderness bequeathed to them by a dead father. The choice before them is restricted and dangerous. To hanker after childhood is a kind of madness. To roam the world means ceaselessly reasserting your independence. It's a well-known fact that Stephie Delacour is a confirmed traveler; the Old Man himself knew that. Sometimes I tell myself that the thought of it might have lightened his last moments, but I'm quite ready to admit this is selfish and presumptuous, because the dying think only of themselves, or of nothing. With the exception, perhaps, of my father, who, like the Old Man, was not of this world and so was able to take an unusual view of it. Unless that's just another illusion on the part of a daughter holding back her tears and half dead with anguish in the dark night of courage that people call a journey.

7

I set out to write a political commentary and stumbled on a detective story. But in the end the death of the Professor, reviving that of my father, brought me close again to myth. No one believes in myths these days, and that includes me. Not to mention my editor, who wouldn't give one houseroom. I don't mind having made the trip for nothing; it isn't the first time. I just wonder whether Father and the Old Man have really reconciled me with myths. Or whether it's just the opposite, and having rediscovered the myths that the two men I loved as a child lived by, and that to my surprise I find they've handed down to me, I haven't emerged from them again into the void. The void of the political hassle my paper keeps going on about. The void of our detective stories, which are full of crime and foolish revolt and hatred. The void of the wandering shape that is myself.

And after all, the Old Man's somber etchings were about the horrors of the world, which, seen from another angle—his own, and that of my father—may be summarized as vanity. *Nothing*, he wrote on his tablet as the flames consumed the myth of resurrection and the face-lifted ones looked on.

But from this void new forms will be born. It's up to you now, Stephie. All things considered, the Old Man may be said to have been delivered from the wolves—I can at least cable that to my paper. And I myself shall set off again with his testament, *Nada*, in search of other metamorphoses.

However, my unspeakable editor will of course want a report. Come on, now—enough of whims and rambling generalizations, we must try to be precise. I shall attempt another hypothesis.

The fact that the President's sympathy (and my own) had led the Old Man to lower his guard shouldn't be underestimated, but it is also true that Septicius died, to all intents and purposes, the day he discovered that not only were the wolves to be found among the invaders, the enemies, the "others," but that their savage makeup was shared by his nearest and dearest, including his own Alba. (Let's leave me out of it for the moment.) He cracked up when he realized there was no longer a Berlin Wall between the wolves and those he loved. This interpenetration of two worlds seen from his own essentially moral point of view as irreconcilable, must, it seems to me, have been the real cause of his death.

Admittedly the misdeeds of Alba and Vespasian are not as infamous as the mass graves and the horrors perpetrated by the hordes from the north. True, a process of domestication is taking place, and soon the wolves won't be mentioned any more, except as if they were a kind of Zulu tribe relegated to some none too secure suburb. The shops in Santa Varvara will fill up with goods again, and I shall be able to get a whisky at the *Oasis* instead of their boring old vodka. Santa Varvara will get more and more like Paris: Vespasian and Alba might easily be from New York or Prague or Clermont-Ferrand, and wouldn't be at all out of place in any of them.

Am I making crime seem commonplace? Is that a way of condoning it? On the contrary, I simply regard it as universal. You might object that there's nothing very spectacular about my thesis, and that it also does away with the suspense so dear to the media and to writers of fiction. I suppose it might be difficult to choose between my humane—too humane—hypothesis of crime as something immanent and perennial, and the idea of it as bestial or insane. The latter is what I'd tend to conclude on the basis of Septicius's grotesque visions. My reason is reluctant to accept them, but I'm unwilling to abandon them for fear of being disloyal. So I shall try to adopt a third theory about crime, which I think would be more to the taste of the Professor and at the same time bring us closer to something like *The Murders in the Rue Morgue.* Poe and Goya—the same insight?

Thus the wolves—with the cunning and ferocity of the orangutans in the rue Morgue, escaped from some tropical clime—took advantage of Vespasian's complicity to get into the hospital. The Face-lifting Colleague let them into the room, the nurses showed them the equipment, and Alba blocked the tube linking the Professor to the artificial lung. Then the beasts destroyed the machine, and with their monstrous claws—I was the only one who noticed marks on his face that couldn't have been made by any human hand— attacked the Old Man's body. The tufts of hair torn out, the congealed blood around his mouth, the marks of strangulation—all bore witness to a savagery of which mere humans are incapable. Vespasian and his Face-lifting Colleague were horrified and tried to disguise the carnage by saying the patient had died of a stroke. I wouldn't go so far as to say they deliberately let the wolves into the hospital out of sheer wickedness: there must have been hordes of the beasts about, to judge by the chaos reigning everywhere when I arrived on that hyper-hygienic scene, though great efforts were being made at a cover-up. But they certainly didn't do anything to keep them out. However, the atrocious scene that was left behind must have passed even their threshold of tolerance. They were disgusted with the murder, and disgusted with themselves. But only subconsciously, I suspect.

8

I almost forgot about the girl who was drowned in the lake, though she was the only certain victim. Of course, to check, I immediately bought a copy of the local rag—*Santa Varvara on Sunday*—and wasn't very surprised to find it very unforthcoming on the subject. "A stranger . . . No one has turned up to claim the unknown young woman whose body was recovered from the lake, drowned as the result of a heart attack." Who were they trying to kid? Who ever heard of a girl falling into a lake as the result of a heart attack? There was still the evidence of the Clean Youth—I'd have to get hold of him somehow—but who would take it seriously? And what about the fang marks? Everyone had seen them. But no one would say anything because everyone was involved in the cover-up. "You were here yesterday or the day before, and saw me in tears? Really? I don't remember anything about it—you must be mistaken. I didn't see anyone!" I can hear them already. No point in beating my head against a brick wall.

Even so . . . The resemblance . . . The nameless victim looked just like Alba Ram: the same face, the same hair, the same Agnes B. suit. I know plastic surgery performs miracles nowadays, but even so . . . It was impossible to believe Alba could have been murdered and a double taken her place . . . Could the person I spoke to at the Old Man's funeral have been merely her double? What about her elliptical way of speaking, which I took to be full of double meanings?—the words wouldn't have had any meaning at all if it wasn't Alba who was talking to me . . . "Stephie is quite intelligent, but she has too much imagination!" (Mother didn't appreciate my wit, having none of her own. But in the present case she might have been right.) Was it just a coincidence? After all, plenty of girls with auburn hair get their clothes from Agnes B., and if you dunked any one of them in muddy water long enough she might easily be taken for Alba or anyone else you cared to name. It was elementary. Was it all due to chance or to necessity? Chance is inevitably objective . . . And so on.

But the fact that the body hadn't been identified was rather disturbing. What we had here was a double who was anonymous: no family or friends, no one whatever to lay claim to Mademoiselle or Madame X, though the Sunday paper knew perfectly well the authorities had a file on everyone, and any policeman, by consulting the records on the computer, could identify a corpse, a suspect, or even an ordinary citizen, without the slightest difficulty. Of course, more and more people were going missing these days, but usually the people concerned were known: it was just that they were looked for and not found. Quite a different matter from the case of the drowned girl. There was no such thing as an unidentified corpse. Or rather, if a corpse was unidentified there was no such thing as a crime.

If you were anonymous you didn't exist. You were nobody. And could anyone commit a crime against nobody? I ask you! In the past the unknown was mysterious, divine, or scientific. But now, in Santa Varvara, the unknown was just a perfect setting for a noncrime. If people weren't wolves they weren't anything. And so there could be deaths, and people could die, but there weren't any murders. There was no anxiety, no dread, no charge, no trial—nothing. No one did anything; everything was blocked by anonymity. I absolutely had to find the Clean Youth. Whether he was a delinquent or not, he'd got the gift of the gab. He might seem stupid, but only enough to confuse everyone.

The mere thought of all this was enough to make me feel as spineless and lethargic as after a course of antibiotics. After all, we didn't know the name of the Clean Youth himself . . . He might be a wolf . . . He might be dead by now . . .

Was I exaggerating? Was I being unduly influenced by the Old Man's pictures? No. The seeming banality of the crime masked a supreme but generalized barbarism, the worst feature of which was that it involved everyone. I ought to bring the wolves and all their accomplices to justice. But I knew what would happen: I'd be confronted with a complete blackout on the part of the authorities: they would turn me into a laughingstock. Wickedness is at its worst when horror is disguised as triviality. It's like everyday life revealing its monstrosities only in dreams or psychoanalysis.

The Old Man wasn't taken in by appearances. He was always analyzing the logic that the cynical and the naive think should be kept secret. Could it be that he died because he looked in the face that which is usually hidden?

9

The airbus descends toward Paris, gray as always under ever lower clouds. At last a bit of coolness. But I still haven't got hold of the murderer.

I fasten my seatbelt and land in the fog, still convinced that although it's possible the murder might have been animal (committed by the wolves), or psychotic (hatched by Vespasian, Alba, and the Face-lifting Colleague), it was really the wiping out of the frontier between good and evil that finally killed Septicius Clarus. A plausible enough theory, but one that can't be proved. I have to go back to the question, What metamorphoses can there be if that frontier no longer exists?

"In nova fert animus mutatas dicere formas corpora." "I made up my mind to tell of the metamorphoses of bodies into other bodies. O gods (for these transformations too were your doing), look kindly on my enterprise, and guide the unfolding of my poem without interruption from the first beginning of the world down to my own day." Ovid too was an optimist. Did he ever so much as envisage the birth of the one true God, in whose light the reigns of Augustus and Tiberius, and the

lives of all other beings since the mists of time, would seem full of impossible monsters and inexplicable events? But there can be no doubt, either for the believer or for the poet: faced with the power of any divinity, whether well-disposed or angry, whether fairy, sorcerer, or magician, human beings are helpless and, in their helplessness, change shape. And their transformation produces a story, and time strikes out henceforward in whatever direction is required of it. But we belong to a different world: one shape is replaced by another, every image blots out its neighbor, and man degenerates into beast through sensational tales, thrillers that don't have the time to tell an original story but merely solve a mystery, a murder tracked down by a modern detective, the Ovid of our modern metamorphoses.

"Taxi! Rue du Cherche-Midi, please!"

A lavender light over the bustling city. A smell of cemeteries or hospitals in my hair—I don't know which. I'm still suspended between two languages. Landing hasn't yet sorted out my memories.

Santa Varvara never did yield me up its secrets.

But I've had enough of all their mysteries, their wolves, their snow, and their jasmine scorched to dust. Of Gulliver's wife and her giant limbs, of the *Oasis* and its cocktails for parvenu ladies, of the military hospital, of face-lifting, of madmen, depressives, manic-depressives, and families slouching in front of the TV. Of trout cooked with ginger, of Alba's auburn lamenting, of Vespasian's sham virility, of death, lakes, beaches, supermarkets, childhood memories, motorways, and of my editor. And of the bunch of lime twigs that the barman thrust in my hands in memory of the Old Man before I left the hotel, and that stink to high heaven here in the taxi that's already stopped in the rue du Cherche-Midi.

Where's the Crime?

Santa Varvara is everywhere. Alba and Vespasian haven't said their last word. Suppose they were still committing their crime at this very moment? But which crime? Perhaps it's a double crime—the simultaneous and reciprocal crime of victim and murderer, who are interchangeable? In fact, if you take into account the deaths of the Girl Without a Name and the Old Man, it's a quadruple murder—which must surely make it a perfect crime? The work of the wolves.

Let them do whatever they like. I shan't lift a finger any more. The murder has left me unscathed. I'm one of them. A wolf. A female wolf who knows what's behind it all and is prepared to talk about it. That's the only difference. Is it a difference at all? Is crime inevitable when there are no more frontiers?

It has started to rain again in Paris. The gray light of evening shrouds the cryptic housefronts in drowsy—should I call it innocent?—inertia. I turn my key in the door with the alert assurance of a detective.

Expect no quarter. I hate the wolves, and now I've got their measure.

DATE DUE

JAN 27 1995	
UPI 261-2505	PRINTED IN U.S.A.